Behind the Station

OTHER WORKS IN DALKEY ARCHIVE PRESS'S
SWISS LITERATURE SERIES

Urs Allemann,
The Old Man and the Bench

Arno Camenisch,
The Alp

Bernard Comment,
The Shadow of Memory

Max Frisch,
I'm Not Stiller
Man in the Holocene

Elisabeth Horem,
The Ring

Luzius Keller, ed.,
Modern and Contemporary Swiss Poetry: An Anthology

Jürg Laederach,
The Whole of Life

Gerhard Meier,
Isle of the Dead

Paul Nizon,
My Year of Love

Giovanni Orelli,
Walaschek's Dream

Noëlle Revaz,
With the Animals

Aglaja Veteranyi,
Why the Child is Cooking in the Polenta

Markus Werner,
Zündel's Exit

Arno Camenisch

Behind the Station

a novel, translated by Donal McLaughlin

DALKEY ARCHIVE PRESS
Champaign / London / Dublin

Originally published in German as
Hinter dem Bahnhof, by Engeler Verlag, Solothurn, 2010

First edition, 2014

Library of Congress Cataloging-in-Publication Data

Camenisch, Arno, 1978-
[Hinter dem bahnhof. English]
Behind the station / Arno Camensnich ; translated by
Donal McLaughlin. -- First Edition.
pages cm.
"Originally published in German as Hinter dem Bahnhof,
by Engeler, 2010"--Title page verso.
ISBN 978-1-56478-335-6 (pbk. : alk. paper)
I. McLaughlin, Donal, 1961- translator. II. Title.

PT2703.A57H5613 2014
833'.92--dc23

2014032101

Donal McLaughlin acknowledges, with gratitude, the receipt
of a grant from the Max Geilinger Foundation in 2013.

swiss arts council
prohelvetia

Partially funded by a grant by the Illinois Arts Council
Published in collaboration with the Swiss Arts Council
Pro Helvetia, Zurich

www.dalkeyarchive.com

Cover: design and composition by Mikhail Iliatov
Printed on permanent/durable and acid-free paper

Behind the Station

Behind the station are the soldiers' cars. We watch as they drive off on Saturday morning and on Sunday evening park their cars behind the station again. They open the car trunks and take out the luggage and the rifles. The rifles have no magazines. We observe how they tie their cravats and do their shirt buttons up. They put on their jackets with the flashes on the shoulders, then their caps, talk to each other as they pass the station and vanish round the bend of the station road.

Gion Baretta lifts the two bunnies out of the box by the ears. He lets them go in the garden. Right, he says, there you go. The bunnies jump around the garden. We jump around after them. Gion Baretta says to my father to wait a few weeks, then they'll be ready, then you can mate them. They clink glasses. My father made the cage. We spread the straw. The bunnies go into the cage. We'll make them a bigger cage later so they've enough room when the bunnies have babies. And see if you don't look after them properly and clean the hutch, we'll be getting rid of them. Off into the pot, understood. We nod. Thanks, eh, my father says to Gion Baretta, don't mention it. Gion Baretta climbs over the fence, gets into his Subaru, and with a wave is gone.

Giacasep lives below us. He has a shop and a tash. He sells screws. He sells nails and chainsaws. He sells hammers, screwdrivers, screw clamps, gas cylinders, tape measures, drills and drill bits. He also sells tool boxes, Mars bars and ice creams. And if you order them, you can also buy bikes from Giacasep. It takes a long time though, for the bikes to arrive, and then the bikes have to be built as well. Giacasep says he'll do it later, he doesn't have time now. He never has time. He has to take screws down into the cellar and he has to make keys. He has a display tower for keys in the shop, he can sit at it on a stool and make them. To do so, he puts on glasses. When Giacasep is making keys, we go through the shop putting fishhooks on each other's pullovers like medals. Near the back entrance he has boxes of nails. In these boxes are nails as long as pencils. The nails have flat heads, the heads of the nails are broad. We stuff nails in our trouser pockets.

On Saturday morning we watch as the soldiers arrive at their cars, untie their cravats, undo their shirt buttons. They open the cars and throw their caps on the back seats. They talk to each other and laugh. In our trouser pockets we have the nails from Giacasep's.

My father asks have we fed the bunny rabbits. We say we'll feed the bunnies in a minute, just need to do something first. My father says, we need to clean the hutch out again soon too. We nod. My father looks strict and shows us his finger. On his finger is white paint. He's wearing overalls. His overalls are white with splashes of paint. My father's a painter. On his shoes are splashes of paint. On his hands are splashes of paint. He's got soap for that that we're not allowed to use. Hands off, my father says, it's poisonous, not for the likes of you. Drink that and you'll end up with a hole in your stomach. We don't want holes in our stomachs so we keep our hands off. My father parks his car at an angle outside Giacasep's shop. Giacasep doesn't like that. Tell your father not to park his car outside my shop. My father's already gone though. He parks and heads up the station road to the restaurant.

My father is in the restaurant. We're behind the station. We walk round the soldiers' parked cars. My brother rhymes off the makes of car. I rhyme off the colours. We kneel at the car doors. My brother kneels at an orange car. I kneel at a red one. With my nail from Giacasep's I draw a house on the side door. My house has a double door. It has a window next to the door and two windows on the upper floor. On the roof there are tiles and a chimney. Smoke is coming from the chimney. I draw curtains in the windows. Next to the house is a garden. In the garden I draw flowers. I also draw a sun and clouds in the sky. In the sky there are two birds. In the garden I draw a big tree. Beneath the tree is a cage. In the cage I draw a bunny.

Next to our house is the Rorers' house. The Rorers don't always live there; they live in Chur and only stay in our village at weekends. The Rorers' house is right beside the railway lines. They never come by train though. They always come by car. Their car is brown. That's an Opel, my brother says. The Rorers can't speak Romansh. When I scrape my knee riding my bike or playing football my mother takes me to Frau Rorer. She's a first aider and paints my knee red, puts on plasters with pictures on them, or bandages it. Come back tomorrow and we'll see then, eh, sweetheart. I nod and she kisses me on the cheek. The frame of her glasses presses into my forehead. I wipe my cheek with my sleeve. My mother then takes her round cherries from the garden.

My mother is complaining. The washing machine has broken down. Boys, she yells, who put nails in the washing machine. My father takes us by the hair; we forgot to take the nails from Giacasep's out of our trouser pockets before throwing the trousers in the tub for dirty clothes. My father pulls at the bottom of your hair at the back. When he pulls it there, it hurts more. Little rogues, my father yells. Ash from his Kiel cigar falls on the rug in the corridor. My father bites on the yellow mouthpiece of his Kiel. His teeth are greyish-yellow. Just you wait, there's going to be trouble, off to bed with you now, no supper tonight: *sez la cuolpa*, only yourselves to blame.

Luis has a steinbock on the sleeve of his blue ski jacket. He's a skiing instructor. He always wears the same jacket and always the same belt as well. Okay boys, he says, if you want some chocolate, nip into the kiosk, into Mena's, and get me a packet of Rössli cigars. Do you know which ones, say it's for Luis and Mena will know, and to put it on the slate. Mena's sitting behind the glass pane, reading the *NewPost*. Behind her, Jesus is hanging on the cross. His right hand's broken off. She takes off her specs and opens the glass pane. What do you want, she asks. Rössli cigars, a Rayon chocolate. Mena won't give us the chocolate, she doesn't believe Luis said we could have the Rayon. She won't give us Torinos either though they're smaller. Luis says, don't worry, you'll get the chocolate from me, bye then, you two. We take the shortcut to the station. Behind the station we discuss it all. It's Mena fault. Mena will be in trouble, we'll take her by the hair.

On Saturday morning the soldiers come down the station road. Do you have any biscuits, we ask. They produce biscuits from their pockets and hold the biscuits out to us. We say merci buccups. They produce dark chocolate from their pockets and hold it out to us. Merci buccups. They laugh and continue down the station road, cutting the bend. You're not supposed to do that. You're not supposed to cut the bend on the station road. When will you finally cotton on that you're not supposed to cut the bend, you little camels, my father says to us, do you want to end up under a car or what. We don't. We only cut the bend when we forget we're not supposed to cut the bend. If we end up under a car, we'll go to Frau Rorer.

Silvana's my girlfriend. She lives above a restaurant, the Crusch Alva. Her mother runs the restaurant. Silvana has a brother, who's bigger than us, and she also has a sister, who's bigger than her brother. Silvana's father's bigger than my father and has hair on his hands and three gold rings on his left hand. My father has a fatter tummy than Silvana's father and paint-spattered hands. I'm in Silvana's bathroom. Silvana's in the bath. She has wet hair and her mother's washing her back. Silvana's mother has rolled up her sleeves. On her left arm she has a watch. It's a Swotch, Silvana told me. Her fingernails are long and red and on her right forearm she has bruises. There's a lot of foam in the bath. I put foam on Silvana's head. She thinks it's funny. I want a Swotch too. Maybe Silvana's mother will give me her Swotch if I take her round cherries from our garden.

My grandmother is bollock naked in front of me. When she sees me, she's startled. She's wide-eyed. She has her mouth open. She hasn't her false teeth in. I'm startled too. I don't look away though. I can't look away. My neck is made of wood. I've never seen Nonna bollock before. She looks so different, totally bollock. Oh, she says. She limps back into the bathroom and closes the door. One of her legs is shorter than the other. The sole of her right shoe is thicker. It looks like she has a wooden foot. But at least she doesn't limp with shoes on. Without her shoes, she stands crooked. Through the bathroom door I hear her say, why didn't you shout something. I don't say anything. I did shout. I shouted *haliho Nonna* as I came in. No one answered. I went into the kitchen with the plastic bag with the mangold leaves from our garden. My mother said to take them to Nonna, Nonna makes her *capuns* with them. I could hear someone in the bathroom, that's why I waited in the kitchen beside the coffee machine. If you want into Nonna's bathroom, you have to go through the kitchen. Nonna comes out of the bathroom. She has tied a bath towel round her. Her toenails are greyish-blue. The bath towel is pink. She doesn't look at me. Why didn't you shout as you came in, silly. I did shout. I don't say so. Suddenly, I can't talk any more. My Nonna, bollock, took my voice away. When she goes into her room and closes the door, I put the plastic bag down on the table beside the coffee machine and leave. I close the front door carefully. There'll be trouble for sure.

My brother lifts the two bunnies out of the cage by the ears. He puts the bunnies down in the grass. Hubert has come with his bunny. It is to mate with our bunnies so there'll then be lots of little bunnies. The bunnies nose at each other and run around each other. We have to give them a little time, Hubert says. The bunnies eat some grass. Hubert takes his bunny by the ears and puts it down beside ours.

The bunnies eat and jump around the garden. Hubert says, what's up, and takes one of our bunnies by the ears. He kneels on the ground and says, hold it tight and push its back legs apart. Get the other one for me, he does the same thing, I hold it tight, you can let go again. Hubert gets up. Those are both bucks, he says. Who'd you get them from, from Gion Baretta, aye in that case.

My bike has a backpedal brake. That's why the pedals move if, when I cycle, I take my feet off the pedals. I backpedal to brake; I don't use the handbrake to brake, it brakes badly. But the backpedal brake, it's good, it leaves black stripes on the asphalt. Today, I'm going down the road to the station for the first time, from the very top, not just the middle like any other time. My brother stands at the bend in the station road and gives me the signal. Legs up and let it roll. As I go, I look down at the pedals, how fast they're turning at this speed, faster and faster they turn till I look up to see I've completed the slope already and am halfway across the square with the post office. I only see Alfons's yellow bus parked in front of me as I go crashing into it. From the ground I can see the dent in the yellow bus. I get up. And then the many scrapes, damn. The front wheel of my bike is bent and I've only had it two weeks. My brother comes running up. Your knee's bleeding, we need to go to Frau Rorer, he says. I try using spit to remove the scrapes on Alfons's yellow bus. There you are, you little bastard. Alfons. He's wearing a beige overall. The overall is fluttering. He raises his hands. He has hands like excavator shovels. I grab hold of my bike with the backpedal brake and take off after my brother. He runs behind the house into the garden, I won't manage to get through with my bike. I run further up the station road and turn off at the garage. Giacasep has left his car out fortunately. I get into the garage easily, put my bike down on the ground and hold the door shut.

Fonsina is Giacasep's wife. She's pregnant. Her stomach is as big as Gion Baretta's stomach. On the first of April, Giacasep says, go into the village shop and get me some MaryLong cigarettes and some Tulihup, Fonsina needs them. He gives me a ten franc note. *MaryLongs e Tulihup*, I say to Marionna in the village shop. She hands me the MaryLongs, and what else, Tulihup, what's that then. Tulihup, Giacasep said, Tulihup. Fonsina needs it. She smirks and says nothing. Phone him if you don't believe me, four one one seven oh, he said Tulihup. She phones Giacasep. She hangs up. She says, we don't have any Tulihup, Giacasep will explain it to you. I'll just take two bottles of Bergamot then, I say. Outside the village shop I put one bottle of Bergamot in my trouser pocket and drink the other in a oner and throw it in the bucket, *voilà*.

Marina's from Italy. She lives above us. Anselmo is Marina's husband. He's an excavator driver and also lives above us.

When Marina cooks, there's a strong smell in the stairs. My brother says she has bad pans. Anselmo has hairs growing out of his ears. The hairs are black. I ask Anselmo can he still hear anything with so much hair in his ears. *Credino maldito*, he says and I run away. When Anselmo says that, it's time to run away. Marina doesn't say things we don't understand. We don't have to run away from Marina. Marina says, *mamma mia*. That, we understand. She says it, for instance, if my brother's lying on the floor in the living room with the living room light in his hand 'cause he climbed onto the table and held on tight to the light to swing across the room. My mother puts her hands up to her mouth and says, fortheloveofgod. She calls Marina and Marina puts her hands up to her mouth and says, *mamma mia*.

Herr Rorer isn't an excavator driver. He looks like a ticket collector. He sits in the garden with Frau Rorer when the sun is shining. They lie beneath a parasol on white collapsible deck chairs, facing the railway lines and counting the trains going up and down the valley. At sixteen past on the dot, the train goes down the valley. At fifty-two on the dot, the train goes up the valley. Herr Rorer has white hair. He also has a white beard and glasses. Herr Rorer gives me his glasses so I can look through them. Through his glasses, everything looks a bit different. He takes a photo of me with his glasses on. He finds that funny. He finds everything funny. He laughs the whole time. I ask him where the cat is. Off to catch mice. He laughs again. Come back this evening, it'll be back by then for sure an' maybe by that time I'll have a sweet for ye.

My grandfather has seven and a half fingers. On his left hand he has five fingers. On his right hand, he has the thumb, the index finger and half a middle finger. The two and a half fingers that are missing, he took off at the big band saw. He wears his wedding ring on the left ring finger. Nonno coughs and says, boys, don't come too close to the band saw on me, or do you want to chop your fingers off. Nonno is the master of the band saw. He needs the band saw to make his rakes, he's a rake maker. Twelve minutes I need to make a rake, he says, from the plank to the finished rake, twelve minutes. Seems Everist made a video of him working back in '81, for the trade fair in Olten. Exactly twelve minutes he needs for a rake. The horn sounds. Telephone.

So you two rascals, Luis says, look what I have here. He shows us the two moles. They're nice and fat eh, caught this morning, still warm nearly, touch them and see. He holds the moles out to us. Their fur is soft and there's dust from the ground on the fur. Why'd you catch them, my brother asks. You're a funny one, why do you think, because they ruin the fields, eat their way through the roots. And look what you do with it. He holds a mole out to me. I take it. Its eyes are teeny. He takes the other mole in his fist and by hand, click, screws its front paws off, then holds his palm out with the mole's two paws on it. Hand them in to the commune, they give you one franc twenty for two paws. Come with me tomorrow and I'll show you how to set the traps, then you can catch moles yourselves and bring them to me and I'll screw their paws off for you. Have you our chocolate, my brother asks. You'll get it alright, eh, but work comes first. He screws the other mole's paws off too, *voilà*, now over to the bridge with you and throw them in the Rhine.

Place on record, my brother says. By the time we're through the whole village, we've counted twenty-five houses, eight hay barns, one car garage, one motorbike garage, the station with the post office, two fountains with the year on them, Nonno's workshop and storeroom, a phone box, Mena's kiosk, and four refuse containers. When we reach the other end, we go through the village again, counting the people who live in the village. We can't count Marionna from the village shop who doesn't live in the village and not Toni Maissen either who stands at the counter in the station but doesn't live in the village either. There are forty-one or forty-two residents. We don't know whether Bollock Tini is one person or two. We need to find out. There are three restaurants in the village, the Crusch Alva where Silvana lives, the station restaurant at the centre, which is closed, and the Helvezia. The Helvezia is my aunt's. There's Marionna's village shop, Gion Bi's Usego store, Giacasep's screws shop, the bakery and the hairdresser's.

Opposite us lives Alexi. He's the village hairdresser. In his hairdressing salon he has three hairdryers. They're for the women. When Alexi has finished cutting their hair, the women have to put their heads under these dryers and wait till Alexi lets them out again. He then uses spray, to keep it in place, he says. So their hairstyles stay in place when the women leave on the train again and stick their heads out the window. When he's finished spraying Alexi says, *voilà*, and holds a mirror up behind the women's heads, is that fine. Only when the women say it is, may they go again. Alexi runs after the women with the handbags they forgot as they rushed to the train. In his breast pocket are hair clips. Only on Saturday mornings do men come to Alexi. They sit on the bench against the wall and slide along till they reach the till. They then know it's their turn next. When we go to Alexi, we have to sit on the bench beside the door with our five franc piece in our hands. We don't get to slide along like the other men. We have to wait till they're done sliding and look at magazines. Alexi pumps the seat up with his foot. His knives tug at our hair. *Fai mal*, does that hurt, Alexi asks. It's okay if it does as long as Alexi doesn't get too close with his bottle of perfume. The bunnies don't like us stinking of perfume. Just a little, to hold it, Alexi says, just a spritz.

Smoke is rising from Nonno's head. What do you two want, he asks, with his left hand behind his back. On you go up to your Nonna, have some elderberry syrup, then go over to the workshop and continue. Yeah yeah, Nonna says. In the workshop, we tap teeth for the rakes. Nonno comes in, puts his earplugs in his ears and turns the band saw on. We have earmuffs over our ears. Above the workshop is Nonno's storeroom. There, he has shafts. He doesn't have the rakes up there, he hides those elsewhere until he attaches the rakes to the shafts and ties them onto the roof of his car and drives off. Almost seventy I've managed to get on the roof at once, he says. In the office beside the phone hangs a photo of him leaning against his car with the rakes tied to the roof. A white car. He has a red one now. For a rake you need seventeen, eighteen, nineteen, twenty, twenty-one, twenty-two or twenty-three teeth. Nonno says he's already made a rake with twenty-nine teeth, that right enough was pretty mad though.

Cuckoo, Rico calls. Rico's at the window beneath the roof with his Flobert rifle at the ready, aiming down at me. He has his left eye closed and is smiling. He has too many teeth in his mouth. His forefinger is on the trigger. I'm going to die. The bag with the eggs from EggToni for my aunt falls on the ground. Rico's about to shoot me. I want to run away. I can't run away. I can't move. My feet are concrete blocks. When you're dead you can't move any more. Dying makes you go stiff. I fall back and bang my head on the road. I hear tooting. It's the angels' trumpets.

When Nonna plays cards, she moves her teeth from side

to side. It makes a bit of a racket. It distracts the other jass players—that's why Nonna's so good at jass. Today, Nonna isn't moving her teeth from side to side. She curses, oh god, *cartas miserablas*, it really is *la miseria*. Boys, Nonna says, go in to Fonsina's and get me my teeth, *cartas miserablas*, dear god. Nonna's teeth are on Fonsina's kitchen table. Don't act so stupid, Fonsina says, one of you will have to take them. Fonsina raises her eyebrows and goes and gets a five franc coin, rests it on the back of her thumb and flips the coin in the air. The coin turns in the air like in slow motion. Pleasepleasedeargod, I'll light a candle for the poor souls.

My brother has Nonna's teeth in his trouser pocket. In his fist, he has the five franc coin. We go through behind the station. Boys, Victor calls. He's at his window. Victor lives on the first floor of the station. He looks like a cat. It's Toni Maissen who should actually live there. Come up here, quick, I've something for you. We both push against Victor's door, you can't open this door without help. How does Victor get into the house, I ask my brother. He says, Toni Maissen helps him with the door. The stairs up to Victor creak. Victor gives us old apples. The skin of the apples is wrinkled like Victor's skin. Where's Luisa, my brother asks. He gives us nuts and lights a cigarette. He smokes cigarettes that aren't tipped: that isn't good for your health. My aunt never smokes cigarettes that aren't tipped, she only smokes Select. When I'm big, I'll only smoke tipped cigarettes. Is Luisa in her room, my brother asks. Victor looks out the window. His eyes shine. We leave. Victor shouts out the window, you forgot the apples and nuts. We'll get them next time.

Silvana's sitting on a stone by the Rhine. Her hair is long and shines in the sun. She's wearing a hair slide. She blinks when I give her the gold ring. I took it from my mother's treasure chest. My mother has eczema on her fingers. She only wears the stag-tooth necklace now that my father gave her for her birthday. Silvana tries the gold ring on each finger. The ring's too big. She gives it back to me. I put it in my trouser pocket. I'll hide it until Silvana's fingers are fat enough. She won't give me the Swotch if I don't give her anything. I'll give her my mother's stag-tooth necklace, then she'll kiss me on the mouth.

The garage is across from the Helvezia. The mechanic is wearing an overall and black mountain boots. The overall's blue and filthy. On his brow the mechanic has a wart and in his hand, an adjustable spanner. The mechanic needs to fix my bike with the backpedal brake. Soon it will be autumn and as soon as it gets colder, my father locks the bikes in Giacasep's barn. The mechanic says, leave it with me and I'll have a look. He has no time. He has to repair Giachen's tractor. You do have time, I say, Giachen's in hospital, he doesn't need his Aebi. Poppycock, says the mechanic. Giachen rolled off into the bushes in his Aebi, my aunt said, with a full load of hay on the back. That's enough, off you go now, the mechanic says. When can I have my bike back, I ask. We'll see, next week maybe. But I need it today. Right, that's it, get lost, the two of you, the mechanic says, or I'll make mincemeat of you.

Do ye not want to come over to play, Frau Rorer asks, Philip's here. But no fighting, eh. Philip comes out of the house. He is Frau Rorer's nephew. He's two years older and a head taller than my brother. Philip also lives in Chur, like the Rorers. When we play with Philip, there's always a fight. If there's a fight and my father sees us, he puts the bunnies on to cook. Philip calls us fuckin' uplanders and gets a roasting for it. Do ye promise not to fight, Frau Rorer asks. I can't promise 'cause if Philip repeats that, there'll be fisticuffs.

We'll be tapping teeth till we're old and have skin like Victor's. Nonno's behind the band saw next to the door, making sure we don't take off. We're the Daltons, breaking stones. We're wearing yellow and black stripes. On our left leg we've a chain with a black ball at the end. The ball's as heavy as a gas cylinder. Nonno is Lucky Luke. He has a blade of grass in his mouth and earplugs in his ears. His cowboy hat he has in the office in the safe. Under his overalls with PTT embroidered on the breast pocket, he has a pistol. He carries his pistol low. Nonno is faster than his shadow. We can't get past him. We'll be tapping till we're grey and have humps like dromedaries from all the tapping. Now and then, a tooth breaks. We throw it into the sawdust and carry on tapping. The evening sun vanishes behind the mountains.

Your Nonno had a blackout while driving, my aunt says, he's to spend a few days in hospital, to be examined, the doctor phoned to say. Then they'll let him out again, my aunt says, your Nonno will soon be back in his workshop and at his band saw with earplugs in, sawing things to bits. And you can help him in the workshop by tapping teeth. He probably won't be able to drive anymore though, Nonno, too risky.

The Rhine gobbles up moles and footballs. The balls get out under the fence and bounce over the stones and into the Rhine. My brother's up to his navel in the Rhine, trying to get our ball back out with a stick. Do you two want to drown eh, Gionclau shouts. He has an axe in his hand. Heavensake, you going to get out of there eh, he shouts. At the end of every sentence Gionclau says eh. If you're speaking to Gionclau, you have to say eh at the end of every sentence too. No, we don't eh, we just need to get our ball out eh. Okay, so get out eh, or do you want a clip round the ear eh. No, Gionclau eh. I hold my hand out to my brother and whisper, Gionclau's coming eh. The Rhine has gobbled up lots of children before eh, Gionclau shouts, don't go thinking eh, you wouldn't be the first eh. He goes over to his barn.

He looks back and shakes his head. We can hear him still grumbling.

My father has put pages from the *Gasetta* down on the living room floor. They cover the whole carpet. My father has his over-trousers on and a paintbrush in his hand. On the floor in front of him is a wooden butter crock. These are used in the alps, boys, to store butter. You'll learn that in time alright, when you're a bit older and have to go up to the alp every summer. On the base of the butter crock my father has drawn our family crest in pencil. He paints in the colours of the crest. We watch him. In his mouth he has a Kiel. Our heraldic animal is the stag. We're a family of huntsmen. When you're older, you two can come hunting too, my father says. That's why on Saturday mornings in the garden he shows us how to shoot, so we'll hit something then.

Gion Bi is the village poet. He lives in the Usego. To the left and right of the Usego he has stacked crates. From the Usego, my mother buys only coffee and eggs from EggToni, you mustn't buy anything else there, she says, all out of date. EggToni drives the eggs to Gion Bi in his Volkswagen Beetle so Gion Bi can sell his eggs. Gion Bi prefers writing to running the Usego, my mother says. My father doesn't like Gion Bi's poems, a pile of crap, he says. I've only ever seen him go into Gion Bi's Usego once. He came back out with an orange racer. It stood behind the house for two months before he took it up the wooden stairs into the barn.

So you two, Gion Bi says. He's at the window on the first floor. Come on up. The bell above the door rings when Silvana pushes it open. And close the door properly or there'll be a draught, eh. In the Usego, there is a light and blue crates with the yellow steinbock on them, the same as my aunt has in the Helvezia. We go up to the first floor. Gion Bi is waiting at the door. He has a fur coat belonging to his dead mother on. On the living room table is a leather handbag with a clasp. That's his mother's too. When he comes into the Helvezia he has the fur coat on and the leather handbag with the clasp with him. In it are his poems, which he takes out once he's seated at the stammtisch, the regulars' table. He takes his horn-rims from his jacket pocket, puts them on and reads out poems till the stammtisch clears and my aunt says, right, that's enough. In here, Gion Bi says, pointing into the kitchen. We sit on the bench. Gion Bi has the same coffee machine as my Nonna. He lifts three small glasses and a bottle. Egg liqueur, he says, it won't kill you, here, drink up.

Nonna looks back, come on, Fido, you slowcoach, get moving. Fido is halfway along. He's walking along the edge of the road, slowly. He won't last much longer, my aunt says when Fido arrives at the Helvezia. She has a cigarette between her fingers and makes a rrrrrrr sound when she exhales the smoke. Nonna's in the Helvezia, laying the jass cloth out on the table. Alexi is seated at the table, shuffling the jass cards. He won't last much longer, Alexi says when Fido goes through the Helvezia. Huh, Nonna asks. She fiddles with her hearing aid. He won't be fit much longer for all this cabaret, Alexi says. What cabaret, Nonna asks. The tags on Fido's collar jingle. My aunt opens the door to the kitchen and Fido goes through the door without looking up. We've put some of Nonna's holy water into Fido's water so he'll want to last long. He goes under the table and lies down beneath the bench. He doesn't come out when we call him. He doesn't hear well any more. To pet him, we crawl under the table.

Outside the byre are Luis and his hay blower, he stuffs in the hay for his three cows and the hay disappears. Where does the hay go, I ask Luis. Up into the sky, through the tube, to the Good Lord. He sticks his hayfork into the haystack on his Rapid. If you have cows one day, he says, you'll need a hay blower too. But be sure not to put your hand in when the propeller's on or it'll tear your arm off. You haven't given us our chocolate yet, my brother says. Not now. In that case—ciao, Luis. If you want your chocolate, stay here and up into the hayloft with you and spread the hay into the corners, I'm not giving you the chocolate for free, you know. And watch you don't stand beneath the tube. Or the hay blower will start to roar again and spit the hay into the byre.

When Luis finally turns the hay blower off, we look like savages, chaff everywhere, look like cannibals from the jungle, which will please my mother no end.

Get me a beer from the cellar, my father says, putting the new cage on two bricks beside the other cage. Hubert has brought us a new bunny, a proper doe, he says, not like the strange ones Gion Baretta has. He has just had it served. The bucks mounted the doe. First one, then the other, then the first one again. Better safe than sorry, Hubert said. It all went ricky-tick. Afterwards they ate grass and jumped around the garden. Now the bunnies are in the cages, looking out. We locked the cages, so whoever wants can come ahead. In the left-hand cage, the two bucks with their brown fur. They're not together though, the cage has a board in the middle and two doors at the front, or else they'd go for each other, my father says. His beer bottle is on top of the doe's cage. The bottle is brown. It's empty. The little bunnies will be here in thirty-one days, Hubert says. That's a helluva long time, my brother says. Every day, on the doe's cage, we etch a mark in the wood with a nail from Giacasep's.

Why do you not go to Mass on Sundays, Nonno asks. He's behind the buffet in the Helvezia with his right hand in his pocket. In his other hand, he has his half a litre. He only drinks half-litres. Nonno looks strict and doesn't look away. He goes to church every Sunday and during the week he goes to the rosary and prays he'll sell a lot of rakes, and that his machines won't chop any more of his fingers off. For that, the priest gives him a cookie. It would do you good maybe to go back to Mass for once, Nonno says. If we went to Mass a lot, we'd be allowed, once we're old and no longer have all our fingers, to go to Chur too and see the Bishop of Chur. I'm on first name terms with the Bishop of Chur, Nonno tells the regulars at the Helvezia, Bishop Vonderach. I must have a word with your mother again, Nonno says. So my mother will tell us to go to church to please Nonno. *Orapronobis*, my father sings.

Marina is moonlighting, my aunt says, but don't tell anyone. That's why she wears colourful headscarves when she's making brochette sticks in Nonno's workshop. She stands at the machine with the tongs with the white handle. The brochette sticks are the same length as sticks for hidings. She lifts the sticks with the tongs and puts them in the machine and takes them out again and puts them in the banana crate. The machine spits the sawdust onto the floor. When Marina pulls the sticks out of the machine, they're the thickness of your finger and round. If a stick breaks, Marina shakes her head and says *merda* or *dio mio* or *porca miseria* and Nonno goes *psst*.

Nonno carries the banana crates with the brochette sticks through the door into the room with the sharpening machine. We used to have a sow in here, Nonno says. These days, it's only Luis who has a sow, and Adolf-dalla-Maria. On the sharpening machine, Nonno makes the brochette sticks spiky. Nonno puts his earplugs in his ears and turns on the sharpening machine. He doesn't let us into the room with the sharpening machine without earmuffs. You'll ruin your ears otherwise, he says, and stay away from the sharpening machine, and don't touch the sanding belt or you'll sand your fingers off up to the knuckles. The brochette sticks now have a point and look like arrows. We fight with them and draw a Z, for Zorro, in the dust on the floor, and if Marina has a break to have an elderberry syrup at Nonna's or smoke cigarettes with Nonno in the boiler room, we tie her scarf round our mouths as we play.

My aunt needs the brochette sticks in the Helvezia, she puts meat on them and Nonna helps her. Nonno cooks the brochettes on Saturday evening on the grill under the tin roof outside the Helvezia. With a ladle, he pours hot oil from a pan over the brochettes and asks the customers, hot or spicy. Nonno fishes out the bits of brochette that have fallen in the oil and says, boys, the bits, and eat up the bread too, not just the meat. If someone has eaten up all his brochette, the bread too, and not stained my aunt's table cloths, he gets to write his name on a slip of paper, fold the slip, and put it through the slit on the lid of the empty hot-chocolate tin. My brother gives the customers the paper and pen and makes sure they put in just one slip and don't cheat. At midnight, we have to open the tin; one of us puts his arm in and takes out a slip. The winner gets a brochette on the house next time.

Nonna's lying in the Helvezia on the couch in the small room, groaning and counting the beads on her rosary. Jeesus, my aunt had shouted when she discovered my Nonna on the floor, and Fido's food. You two need to leave now, my aunt says when the doctors come. They put cables in Nonna's arms and lay her on a board, carry her out of the Helvezia and put her in the trunk of the ambulance. My aunt gets to sit in the front. The ambulance drives off. The doctors have forgotten to put the siren on. Nonno coughs and stays behind in the Helvezia, or else someone will nick my aunt's wallet from the drawer beside the coffee machine.

My father's rifles are leaning in the wardrobe in the bedroom, behind my mother's clothes in the right-hand corner. There are four rifles: the Flobert, the military rifle, the small-game hunting rifle with two barrels, and the stag rifle. The cartridges he has hidden elsewhere. If my father's not at home and my mother isn't either, we take my father's stag rifle out of the wardrobe. This rifle is bigger and heavier than the others, a proper rifle with ornaments on it. We lie on the rug in the corridor with the stag rifle and aim at the animals. We are my father in the forest and are wearing his hunting vest and his hunting cap and have the butt of a Kiel in our mouths with a yellow mouthpiece. *Pif paf*, drop dead.

Frau Muoth drives a Volkswagen Beetle. The Volkswagen Beetle is white. And she has a grey perm, which Alexi did for her with his hairdryer. Frau Muoth doesn't speak Romansh, just German; she doesn't have to be able to speak Romansh, she almost never speaks and so can say what she says in German, the people in the village understand that too. Frau Muoth has bees. She has her bees at the edge of the village. Every day, at a quarter to twelve on the dot, Frau Muoth drives through the village in her Volkswagen Beetle. She drives fast and if she's coming we've to make sure to stand to the side. Frau Muoth is older than my Nonna. She can't see so well any more. The seat in her Volkswagen Beetle doesn't have a backrest, that's why she leans forward as she drives. Her thick glasses don't help any either, my aunt says, so make sure you're not on the road when you hear her coming. You can hear her from afar. Her Volkswagen Beetle is so noisy, the mechanic says, 'cause Frau Muoth only drives in first gear. At a quarter to twelve on the dot the people in the village step off the road as Frau Muoth rockets through the village to get to her bees. At a quarter past one on the dot the people stand to the side again. Frau Muoth drives through the village in the other direction.

My mother takes us with her to the hospital in Chur. Kindly drive safely, my father said. We're going to visit my Nonna in Chur. Her leg is kaput, my aunt said. She's in a bed in Room 303, watching TV. In her room are three other women. Nonna's the oldest. Look who it is, Nonna says with a smile when we go in. It smells of old apples in the room. My mother hides the bottle of schnapps for Nonna and the schnapps glass in the top drawer of her bedside table. Nonna likes her small schnapps in the evening, my mother says, the doctors mustn't know. Nonna drinks on the side. On Nonna's bedside table are her rosary beads and a prayer book and the *NewPost*. Nonna's lying in bed in a white blouse. Her whole leg is in plaster. The cables coming from her arm are linked to a plastic bag hanging on a clothes tree. In the plastic bag is elderberry syrup. Those are beautiful flowers, Nonna says, you shouldn't have though. She looks out the window. She has shiny eyes. The nurse puts the flowers in a vase.

Holygod, what kept you so long, my father asks. We went shopping as well, to Vögeli and ABM. My mother boxed our ears in Vögeli for crawling among the clothes rails, playing tag. I'm never going to Chur with those two rascals again. People must've thought we're savages up here. There'll be no supper tonight and an early bedtime. To teach us a lesson, my mother has bought us shoes that are too big. We look like clowns in them. You'll grow into them, I'm sure, and that's the end of it, don't think I'm going to buy you new ones every two weeks. She has stuffed newspapers into the toes.

Frau Rorer, where were ye, my brother asks, we were in Chur and hid schnapps in Nonna's bedside table and didn't see you. Well well, says Frau Rorer. She takes her glasses off and comes over to the fence. So why's Nonna in Chur, is she in hospital, is she ill then. Her leg's kaput and she's lying in hospital, has to wear a white blouse and gets to watch TV all day. Oh that's not so good, Frau Rorer says. Our mother's always saying that too, not to watch so much TV. We'd understand alright if we suddenly needed glasses, only ourselves to blame we'd have, *sez la cuolpa*. Frau Rorer has only herself to blame too. She should've eaten more carrots and watched less TV. In that case, I'll need to go and visit Nonna, Frau Rorer says, and play *Ciao Sepp* with her, she really enjoys that.

No one in the village has locked their front door. We tried every house in the village, not a single front door was closed; only Toni Maissen's door at the station was, Marionna's shop and the Rorers' house. I don't get why Giacasep has a key tower if no one needs a key, apart from Toni Maissen and Marionna and the Rorers.

From now on, I'm the sheriff in the village and every time you see me you have to say hi sheriff, Silvana's brother says. I shake my head and he lunges out and cuts a hole in my head with the big garden hoe. Frau Rorer needs a long time to patch my head up again. The blood's sticking to my hair and she puts the scissors away again when I kick out with my feet. It's not as bad as I first thought, she says, eat radishes and it'll get better quicker. I don't like radishes. I'd rather run around with a hole in my head. If I rub my hand over my head, I can feel the hole. There'll be revenge for this.

A bell rings at the station before the train's due so Toni Maissen can stop doing crosswords and prepare. He comes out of the station too late and the train has to wait 'cause Toni Maissen still has to give people the tickets he takes from the drawer and pushes under the glass pane. You're just half portions, he says, cutting the cardboard tickets for children in two with the big scissors. The conductor raises his hand, *Saluti*, blows the whistle and only gets on properly when the train's already moving. Once the train disappears, Toni Maissen takes off his police cap and goes back into the station. He puts the cap on the desk at the big window with green and red lines on it. There it remains till the next train comes. If I was Toni Maissen, I'd wear the cap all day.

Gieri trains the big ones. They play in the league with the men from the neighbouring village. There aren't enough players in our village 'cause you need eleven and not just six like for the Grümpi tournament. After Mass on Sunday everyone waits on the square outside the church. Gieri's not in a hurry. He has his little chats with people before finally going to the notice board. He takes a slip of paper from his jacket pocket and tacks his team for the game that afternoon to the notice board. The people crowd round Gieri. Gion's the sweeper yet again, Mena says to Gieri, I don't get it, he can't head the ball, that one. And Bighi, Alexi says, is a striker, not a defender. Spare me your gripes, Gieri says, I'm trying things out. Gaudenz is on the substitutes' bench. He didn't go to church. When we're big and playing in the championship, we'll go to church every Sunday for sure.

How often have I told you, my mother says, not to play football in the kitchen. Where can we play football: not against the station or Toni Maissen comes out to complain; not in the garden where Marina has to hang out her sheets, then tells Anselmo we dirtied them. Anselmo then comes out and forces our heads down into the sandpit, where the cats shit. If we play football on the football pitch, Gionclau comes out with his axe eh and says eh you'd better go home eh, you good-for-nothings. We're not allowed to play in the street 'cause Frau Muoth will run us over, and if we play football in the kitchen, my mother says we're camels.

Now that Nonna's in Chur, Nonno doesn't have to hide in the boiler room with his cigarette. Behind Nonno's workshop is the forest. A few tree branches stretch over the roof of the workshop. On one side of the workshop, steps go up into the forest. Before you get to the forest, the storeroom's on the right. This room has no doors and is directly above the room with the sharpening machine where Nonno makes the brochette sticks spiky and the sow used to be. He hasn't hidden his rakes here but he has a lot of junk here. Don't be going up there, you've no business up there. In the storeroom are crates and old tools, handles for the scythes and wooden plates that deer horns and chamois horns will be stuck onto. For a stag's horns, the plates are too small. We find a ladder against the wall and climb up into the second floor of the storeroom. Up here are three large coffins and a child's coffin made of bright wood. The coffins are locked. Open them, my brother says. There are dead people in the coffins for sure.

The big one there, my brother says. On the side of the coffin are two keys. I turn one key and my brother the other. Ants crawl out of my mouth and over my face. We open the lid. The coffin's empty. My brother lies down in the coffin, joins his hands, shuts his eyes and says, close it.

Nonna was given crutches at the hospital that lean against the chair 'cause she just lies on the couch all day. I can't even cook any more, she says. Nonna likes to cook, she cooks hot and spicy and always too little. Exactly the right amount again, she says, when the bowls on the table are empty. And if there's still something left in the bowls, she says, who'll have that little bit, we wouldn't want to leave it. Boys, come on, eat some more, eat the little that's left and save a soul.

So you two chappies, Otto says, did you two scoff the Torinos in my fridge. He has a beard like a shovel. Yes, says my brother, the chocolate marshmallows too. Kindly ask the next time eh, Otto says, doesn't cost anything to ask. I don't want some night to be desperate suddenly for a piece of chocolate again and have to go to Gion Bi's for more 'cause you two raided my fridge. You'll have to pay me back though eh, I've a task for you. The time we broke the handle of the wheelbarrow, when it rolled down the slope on us with Fido in it, we were tasked with counting how many cats there are in the village, how many dogs and how many hydrants. There were thirteen cats and six dogs, four hydrants. Right, pay attention, Otto says, the task is: tell me at noon tomorrow, here, the names of all our mountains.

There are sixteen fridges in the village.

My brother looks like an Arab. He has a turban on his head 'cause Balzer from the next village drove over him on his motorbike. My brother was on the station square with his bike, behind the yellow bus, when along came Balzer on his Kawasaki, much too fast and with no helmet on. The doctors patched up his head and put the turban on and he has to wear it now until the small game hunting is over. I've told my father it was Balzer so my father can beat him up.

Nonna can't get to Mass 'cause of her leg. The priest's coming tomorrow, Nonna says to my aunt. Don't know about that, my aunt says, drawing on her Select, he can't be, the priest always comes on Mondays and not Thursdays, rrrrrrr, tomorrow Dr Tomaschett's coming. The priest's coming tomorrow to give me extreme unction, he'll maybe bring a few communion wafers too, says Nonna. What are you on about, the doctor's coming tomorrow, to give you your flu jab, at half past eleven. I'd rather the priest came tomorrow with the oils, Nonna says, much rather that than Tomaschett.

Early in the morning, Otto cycles off to hunt. His bike is silvery, a racer, my aunt says; that's not right though, it's a semi-racer with a luggage rack and ten gears. On his back he has his rucksack, with the barrel of his shotgun peeking out, and his binoculars are dangling round his neck. He hides in the bushes and only now and then can you see the glow of his cigarettes. Patient as a tree stump, he crouches in there all day. If it gets dark and Otto has yet to fire a shot, he comes out of his bushes and fetches his semi-racer that is leaning against a tree on the forest road. He cycles back to the village, to right outside the Helvezia, where he parks his semi-racer beside the entrance and says nowt. Don't shoot and you don't miss.

The hind's lying outside Alexi's hairdressing salon and we're kneeling behind it. The hind has a fir branch in its mouth, dry eyes, and a hole in its neck you could put a finger into. My brother holds it by the ears for the photo my mother's taking with my aunt's camera. Look over here, my father says from behind my mother. The stag gun is against the hind's stomach, with the barrel pointing up. I could look down it but am not allowed to 'cause I've to look at the camera. My mother presses the orange button and the camera spits the picture out, she takes the photo and waves it to and fro and we appear in the picture with the hind outside Alexi's salon. My brother looks funny with the head bandage. All that's missing is a white sheet or drape and a black tash and he'd be a proper Arab.

Giacasep has parked his car outside the Helvezia, behind it at the exhaust is Nonno's green suitcase. What does it say on his case, I ask my aunt, *Passugger*, she says, Nonno has to go away for a few days. Is he going to see Vonderach, I ask. No, he has to go to hospital. Yet again—he's just been. The doctor said he needs to go in for another few days; he has black marks in his chest. Giacasep and Nonno come out of the Helvezia and my aunt stubs her cigarette out with her foot. Nonno stops in front of us, and his fingers reach into the front of our hair. He makes a cross on our foreheads with his thumb.

My uncle has bushy sideburns and drives an orange Citroën. In his Citroën hangs a Magic Tree with naked women on it. He drives fast and when the sun's shining, he takes us and Fido with him. He puts his pilot's glasses on and rolls the roof back and we stand on the back seat, holding on tight to the rod down the middle of the roof. The wind blows our hair back and we let go with one hand on straight bits. My uncle laughs, glances at the road, then back up at us again. Fido's on the front seat. My uncle strokes his ears when he whines and holds on tight to his collar on bends. On bends, the Citroën squeals and slants, almost tipping over.

Outside the Helvezia is Luis's car. The trunk of his Subaru is open, and in it is a stag. Its head's hanging out over the bumper bar and blood's dripping from its mouth to the ground. In its mouth, the stag has a fir branch. So you two gunmen, Luis says, just look eh, enormous this one is, over one eighty for certain, quite certain, you don't get one like that in every lifetime, this one's major. He takes the stag by the head, hunters on their bikes like Otto can only dream of one like this. It's got perfect antlers, a double crown, see that, forget how good the *Pfeffer* made from this one might taste, you can probably eat it raw, that's how good it must be, and the ball-sack, a ball-sack the size of a haversack this one has. He opens the stag's mouth and raises its lips. And look at these teeth, see those, I've rarely seen such healthy teeth.

Bollock Tini lives across from the Usego. He stands outside his house with his hands in his trouser pockets. The cigar in his mouth is like a cork. He has a French beret on his head and raises his head when he sees us. Ciao, Bollock Tini, we say, moving on quickly. My mother said we're not to go to Bollock Tini's. We need to drop by actually to ask is he one person or two. But we don't want to drop by 'cause my mother also said that in the old days Bollock Tini would take children along to make hay and make them show him their peckers. In return, he shows his pecker too on Sundays: when the people come out of Mass, Bollock Tini's always bollock on his balcony.

Twenty-seven marks have been etched on the doe's cage. In the morning and at noon and in the evening, we look to see if the doe has finally made the babies. But there's nothing lying in the straw yet. She's made a proper nest in the corner and is sitting in it, eating pears and potato peelings. And she's got so fat she wouldn't be able to jump around the garden any more. We don't let her out either, or someone will shoot her through the ear. My mother said, in the hunting season hunters get confused from all that shooting, so best leave the doe in the cage.

The year you were born, I shot the biggest stag, my father says, a stag the size of a monument. Its antlers are hanging in the corridor beside the butter tub with our family crest and reach to the ceiling nearly. In the forest up on the spring pasture I sat very quietly on a stone covered with moss and waited, my father says and his eyes shine, know what, when a king like that is close, you sense it, it tickles your tongue. The jay high in the fir tree gave a screech and I knew he's on his way now and raised my gun. No way did I tremble, not a bit, was like I'd turned to stone. Suddenly he appears in the clearing, a giant, and I didn't study anything, just bang, headshot, and he fell to his knees.

Next to the Helvezia lives Maria, and Adolf-dalla-Maria. He has a goat on a chain in the stable that he never lets out. Adolf-dalla-Maria isn't at home and we climb over the stable door into his dark stable and give the goat courgettes from Frau Rorer's garden. While it's eating we kneel at its udder and squirt milk into each other's mouths till the goat kicks out with its hind legs, lifts its tail and shits Maltesers. Out of here, *hopp*, Adolf-dalla-Maria shouts. He's in the doorway, blocking it so we can't get past. We hide behind the goat. He's going to chain us up on all fours beside the goat and won't let us out again and we'll have to eat hay till we're old and die, or he'll tear us in half and feed us to his sow.

The first banana in the village, was Gion Bi had it, my aunt tells the regulars at the stammtisch, and he ate it skin and all. He couldn't have known, Alexi says, we'd all have done the same, eaten the skin and all, you didn't know any better in the old days. He takes his snot rag from his trouser pocket and blows his nose. You know, kids, he says to us, we've not had bananas for that long here. In the old days, you'd polenta every day and potatoes and cheese and every now and then some sausage, but no bananas. And nowadays there are so many bananas in the valley, as if bananas grew in our forests, bananas day and night, as many as you want, as if even our forefathers had only eaten bananas, it's true, I'm telling ye.

I met Toni Maissen this morning, my mother says, told me

I should lock you two up or put you in a home so you'll finally learn maybe and stop your nonsense. In there, he said, they'd nobble you two and soon put a stop to all your nonsense if I can't rear you myself, or else you'll end up as criminals, that's what he said. So do you want to go into a home, she asks, wiping her tears. And I met Adolf-dalla-Maria yesterday and do you know what he said, the next time he'll take the carpet beater to you and you won't be able to sit down for three weeks. And if I tell your father you took his rifles out of the wardrobe, you know what'll happen. She sits down on the floor with her back to the wall in the corridor under the big stag. She has her hands over her face. We go over to her. She holds us tight.

Fonsina has to go into hospital or her stomach will burst. The baby's not here yet though, it isn't days later either, and we ask my mother why Fonsina went in so early if she now has to wait in the hospital, instead of staying in Giacasep's shop and counting screws. My mother says the baby will come out one day and then it doesn't and people don't know exactly. Fonsina has a sore stomach 'cause of it and now has to lie and it's better for her not to do anything. Did we cause that much trouble too, my brother asks. You, you kept still the whole time, for nine months, then knocked on the door on the very day, the very one, my mother says to my brother, and out you came without any ballyhoo and at a speed that had them all marvelling. You though, you'd no patience, wanted out after only four months and caused a whole spectacle. The doctors said I'd just have to go into hospital, like Fonsina now too. Five months I lay in a hospital bed, waiting, with nineteen pills to take a day.

Otto, have you never shot a stag or what, my brother asks in Otto's corridor where there's not a single antler on display. I have indeed, says Otto, have shot a whole dozen already, I shoot a beauty every leap year. So why've you not hung the antlers up, I ask. I ask myself that, says Otto, let them display who have to.

Lucas is on the station square and not moving. Alfons, in his yellow bus, can toot as much as he wants, Lucas isn't for moving. He moves his ears back and forth. Giacasep pulls the rope and Anselmo pushes from behind, nothing doing though. Go over to Herr Rorer and get a few carrots, Toni Maissen says to my brother, and you, run into the Helvezia and tell Giachen that Lucas is blocking the square outside the post office and to kindly come and get him, and today rather than tomorrow.

I'd give him even more candy, the dentist in Disentis told my mother, lots of choc and candy, daily's best, it's not a bit of wonder he has teeth like an old horse. Mine would hurt too if I'd teeth like that, they'll all fall out on him soon, if things continue like that, and the dentist would have to work miracles again, like he was the dear Lord himself eh. Next Wednesday again, but be punctual this time, he said, closing the door. On the train home, I sit at the window and my mother gives me Tridents to chew that she bought at the kiosk in Disentis and says, an Alcazil this evening and you'll sleep like a slipper, and tomorrow morning, along to the Crusch Alva with you, Dr Tomaschett's there on Thursday mornings in the small dining room, he doesn't make such a ballyhoo and then all will be well.

Anselmo's sitting in the bath with a cigar butt in his mouth. One arm's hanging over the edge. The smoke hangs like fog beneath the ceiling. Anselmo and Marina's bath is the smallest in the whole village. Anselmo sits in it like he was in a car. He leans the back of his head against the wall and the water's up to his chest, which is covered with a black carpet that reaches under his arms. Round his neck he has a gold chain. *Fuori bastardi*, Anselmo says, gesticulating. He turns up the radio with the bent aerial on the washing machine beside the bath and draws on his cigar. The smoke rises slowly like a wisp of cloud. The radio's playing Italian songs and once we're out of the bathroom, we hear him singing along, *senzatee, se-enzat-ee*.

Twelve little bunnies the doe made on Sunday morning. They lie close together in the straw behind the doe and are teeny. They've their eyes closed and don't have any fur yet but the little ones' fur will be grey for sure and brown and black and black-and-white and white. Twelve is a helluva lot, my brother says, a doe's never made that many at once before, for sure. She gets more food specially today, hay and cucumbers and tomatoes from Frau Rorer's garden. We cover the little ones with straw again and take our hands out of the cage so the doe will stop scratching the bottom of the cage.

Nonno's back from hospital. Praisebetothelord, Nonna says.

In the Crusch Alva, I've to wait on the bench in the corner under the medal cabinet, thinking of the jam omelettes my mother's making me today. Silvana's sitting beside me, playing Happy Families with me, with wild animals. I'm the last to be seen, only after Alexi has been in the small room with the doctor, then Gion Bi, Gion Baretta, Mena, the mechanic, EggToni, Marionna, Victor and the baker. *Soli*, just the young man left, Dr Tomaschett says, holding the door for me, then that'll be it again for this week. He's wearing a black suit and on the table is a leather case. Let me see your misery, he says, adjusting his glasses on his nose. Aha, opens his case and takes out the pliers. No one has died of that yet, just so you know, first though, drink this, he says, handing me the glass before plunging the pliers into my mouth.

Can you see the antennas on my head, Gion Bi asks, open your eyes wide, have a good look, you can believe me alright, you as well, I can see it, you've these antennas too, not everyone has them, only very few people have them, in your case though I can see them quite well, fine, thin, beautiful antennas growing out of your head, it's just they're still so thin you haven't noticed yet that antennas are growing out of your head too. Only once you're older and bigger and have more wrinkles from lots of thinking and looking like me, only then will you see the antennas. Not everyone can see them, only those who have antennas themselves can see them. You just have to watch no one breaks them on you, you'll need them 'cause, believe me, you'll know soon enough what for, when the time's right eh. Know what I mean. I shake my head. Doesn't matter, *au revoir*.

Lucas has been run over, my aunt tells Giacasep at the Stammtisch. Yes, last night, was standing on the road on the bridge after the bend when along came Luis like a nutcase in his Subaru and went over him, dead on the spot, nothing you could've done to help. Luis was here till after midnight, oiling himself a bit. Just leave the Subaru here, I even told him, you've not got far to go, just to be on the safe side, that's what you think, he said though, anything else, then got into the car and slammed the foot down. Fine by me, Giachen said.

It's raining. Silvana has had to put her red raincoat on and her boots too. We want to show her the new bunnies and tell her about how we let all the bunnies jump around the garden, how they eat all the grass, and how we need to let them into Frau Rorer's garden too so they have their fill, how all the new bunnies will have babies too and we'll need a big barn for the hundreds of bunnies, and a lot of cages that we'll let her help to build. When we get to the cage the doe's alone in the cage. The babies have vanished. They're not under the straw, not in the corners, not on the ground in front of the cage, not behind the cage, not in the garden and nowhere at all. They're gone.

Luis has stolen the little bunnies for sure, has screwed their paws off and handed them in to the commune, my brother says, or Gionclau eh, has used them to make pies eh, or Anselmo has given them to Marina for her birthday and she's made mince with them to go with the spaghetti, or Adolf-dalla-Maria has torn them to pieces and fed them to his sow, or Mena has made jam with them and filled them into jars. Hey, is someone in the container, Hubert asks, lifting the lid, what are you up to in here. We need to work out who has nicked our bunnies. Twelve babies the doe made on Sunday morning, and now they're gone. So do you not want out of the container. Not until we've found out who has stolen our bunnies. So did you put your paws in, Hubert asks, and did you maybe stroke the babies and take them out and hold them. No, that's not good, not good at all, no, if you did that then *sez la cuolpa*, the doe has eaten them.

Nonno's sitting in his beige PTT-overalls with wood chips in the pockets at the table in the kitchen. Nonna brings him a bowl of steaming coffee, sits down beside the coffee machine and with her hands joined mumbles rhymes with Nonno. They make the sign of the cross and lift their spoons. Nonno tears pieces of the loaf off and puts them in the bowl. With his spoon, he presses the pieces into the milky coffee and fishes them out again. Even as a little boy Nonno used to do that, Nonna says, a habit you can't correct. Make sure, lads, you don't start this kind of habit too—a bit of hard bread from time to time doesn't do any harm.

At the baker's, it smells so good. He lives on the other side of the road beside the station restaurant. Through the shop window you can see him with his baker's peel; thin, and so big he has to duck. His bakery's much too small for him. He's so big 'cause he eats too much panforte. He gives us plum rolls for free. Luzia's his wife. She stands behind the vitrine on a wooden stool and asks, what will it be today then.

It's the Helvezia's birthday—it's a hundred years old. My aunt has decorated the Helvezia with garlands; they're hanging above the door, on the door and round the windows, garlands in all different colours. The celebration will be fabulous, said Giacasep, who helped put up the platform for the politician from the next village who is coming to tell stories about the Helvezia. Straight out of a fairy-tale book he is, with his big shoes and red nose. The Swiss flag is hanging on the platform. When evening comes and all the people from the village arrive, all the food is ready in the Helvezia and the band lines up in the car park. The conductor moves his hand and his little stick, and the band plays the birthday march. They play three beautiful songs next and the people applaud and they lay their instruments aside and sit down at the tables. It's time for the politician, Giachen says to Giacasep, let's see what he's going to say this time. We'd have more to say about the Helvezia than this guy presumably, he says. That's prestige for you, at celebrations you have to let the *politicus* speak. The guy in the tie speaks so helluva long that Nonna shouts out that the people are hungry. At the end, my aunt gets a bouquet of flowers and kisses, puts the bouquet in the kitchen beside the meat grinder, and, ready-steady-go, the guzzling commences.

Fridolin is the name of Fonsina's baby. He's lying in his cradle in the living room, asleep. He's not any bigger than a white loaf and I don't dare touch him or Fonsina will gobble him up. When the baby wakes, he screams so much the window panes shake. He's hungry, Fonsina says, and takes Fridolin out of the cradle, saying na na, and she breast-feeds him till he falls asleep again or she carries him round, singing the ladybird song to him. Fridolin's hands are still so small and look like moles' paws. If Fonsina holds out her finger to him, he takes the finger in his paw. If I stick my tongue out at him, he sticks his tongue out at me too.

My father has locked our bikes in Giacasep's barn and we're not allowed to run round in gym shoes any more, it's gradually getting cold after all, during the day too, my mother said. My brother's been allowed to take off the turban. He looks almost the same as before, it's just he has no hair at the back of his head. He now has a zip there instead. Alexi cuts his hair short, a boy's haircut; looks quite decent now, he says. In the morning there's frost in the garden and the bunnies are no longer allowed out. In the cages are tufts of fur. They're blowing their coats, my father said, are getting ready for winter. In the winter they've longer fur, or else they'd be cold in the cage out in the garden. We spread a lot of straw in the cage, and hay too so it's nice and warm for them.

Silvana and I are in the barn, playing *Mund sutsu*, upside-down world. You play it with tarot cards. Each player has ten cards in his hand and has to put one down. The player with the highest card takes both until one of us has none left and has lost. The highest card is the World, it beats all the other cards but one, and on the World there are two X's at the top. The lowest card is the Bagat with an *I* at the top. He looks like a chicken keeper. Only the Bagat can beat the World, he is the strongest card.

At midnight, there's a terribly loud and peculiar sound and roar in the village, it sounds like the sirens of the fire brigade, only much louder, chasing the people of the village out of their houses in the middle of the night, onto the station square. They stand there in the dark, staring up at Grep Ner, the rock in the middle of the forest, where flames are licking out, like a dragon was spitting fire up there. Otto is on Grep Ner, putting on a spectacle with his fire organ.

The sun has disappeared and will only return in three months. Like every other year, it shone for the last time on the station square bang on the eighth of November, my aunt, looking serious, says at the stammtisch; we're now in the shade and it's getting cold too. The three months will pass too, no doubt, dress warmly, Alexi says, on the eleventh of February it will return again and then it will soon be spring. A likely story, I wouldn't be too sure, Otto says, raising his forefinger, this year isn't every year, I've observed the sun's path. Him and his theories again, Alexi says, gesticulating. Oh you're right to hesitate, the sun has changed its path, it didn't disappear this year the same way as other years. Aha, slowly but surely you're going mad, Alexi says, turning his beer bottle. Let's see then, eh, who's thinning out a bit at the top, Otto says, in recent years the sun disappeared right behind the tops of the firs on Grep Ner, not this year, I swear. I wouldn't be so sure that it'll return, eh, *pagar*, can I pay, got to go.

What's up with Otto, about to do a rain dance maybe, Giachen asks my aunt at the stammtisch, he was a bit flustered just now, hardly said hello, not even time for a chat, in a hurry he was, out of the way, he said and set off on his racer up to the forest. My aunt shrugs her shoulders and draws on her cigarette, don't know, she says, he was talking about the sun and something going wrong there, rrrrrrr, seems it didn't disappear the same way this year as other years. Oh, *pulaccas,* bunkum, Alexi says, aims for the chalet and doesn't even hit the alp.

Finally, I can go along the main road again if I want to go to the Helvezia. Rico's no longer at the window under the roof with his Flobert. He's moved away, my aunt said, to the lowlands, to do an apprenticeship as a motorbike mechanic. We saw him standing at the station with three suitcases and smoking cigarettes. When the train came, he got on and sat at the window. Toni Maissen waved bye-bye to him.

My mother's won five hundred francs. She bought a lottery ticket at the kiosk from Mena, like she does every week, and didn't she go and win. She stands in the living room, holding up her ticket, I've never won anything and now five hundred francs. We're rich, I've never seen so much money all at once—my mother will buy herself something big with it. Maybe she'll buy us a tractor, then we could all drive it in the garden. We'll use it to buy a microwave, she says though, one the same as Nonna's, a brown one with two black screws on it and three white buttons.

At the stammtisch in the Helvezia at least one cigarette is always lit. We'll stick to the fire in winter, if the sun's not going to come to us, my aunt says and smirks. The glow of the cigarettes looks like the eternal light in the church. It's behind the priest's high desk, where the stairs go up to the viewing tower, in a white bird's cage on the wall. It burns orange and must never go out, the priest explained, the eternal light is a symbol of the Good Lord, of him being among us and protecting us. In the Helvezia the eternal light mustn't go out either. In winter, even more eternal lights get lit than usual; almost all the people in the village join in, light cigarettes and smoke and smoke. They light lights for the poor souls, so we'll remain well and the sun will return and no one goes batty.

During the night, my father comes into our room and wakes us. He sits on the edge of the bed to explain to us what's good and what's not, who's good and who isn't, who is sound and who's a fuckin' bastard and why you should run over someone like that. He goes from one bed to the other, beaming and laughing, then starts to cry again, waves his hands, speaks in rhyme and sings, curses quite loud, farts, and says whoops. The fish in his mouth swims through his words

Didn't see you two at Mass, Nonno says, maybe you weren't there again, heavensake, a disgrace it is. Not even on Sundays do you go regularly, what's to become of you, you'll turn into heathens on me yet, you two, but is it any wonder, like father like son, and if the father doesn't go, the brats don't either. It was different in the old days, ask your mother. In the old days, we wouldn't've dared not go to Mass, says Nonno. We went to church every day and went willingly, let me tell you. Every morning at seven there was a Mass, day in day out, summer and winter. On Sundays, up to five times, once in the early morning, once in the morning, at noon, in the afternoon and then you went to the rosary in the evening, that's how it was. The priest checked was everyone there. If anyone was absent, he always noticed; something best avoided, or else wallop wallop, you got a clout on the left and a clout on the right, and a few more from your mother and father on top of that in God's name.

What are heathens, my brother asks Otto, Nonno said we're turning into heathens. Heathens, zounds, you'll have to find that out yourselves.

In Gion B's apartment there are pages everywhere. In the middle of the table is a typewriter and a table lamp. At the table sits Gion Bi in his fur coat. He has brown suede slippers on, and his horn-rims on his nose. His head's leaning forward and he's asleep. *Salut* Gion Bi, Silvana says, what you doing. Oh, did I leave the door open, Gion Bi asks, you're allowed to knock, you know, instead of giving people a fright. What you doing, Silvana asks. Writing poetry, *cara*. And why have you so many pages on the floor. Know what, *poesia* is a curse, you study it till your head's empty, till it has nothing left in it and doesn't notice the day passing at all. Then in the evening, when I get up from my chair, I see all the paper round the floor, like two wolves had been in here.

Will you read us a *poesia*, Silvana asks. Only once it's finished, it'll take a while. Right, I need to continue, it's already late, off you go now.

In a corner in the Helvezia an old man is sitting. On his head he has a hat that is full of dust. His grey eyes look out from under the hat. From time to time he rubs his nose. His shovel's against the wall. It's Fazandin. He sits in that corner every day. My aunt says, what kind of nonsense are you talking, there's no one sitting there. But that's not right, Fazandin sits there every day, today as well. My Nonna says, you'll end up making me afraid. There's no need for her to be afraid of Fazandin. Only Otto believes me. He says, yes yes, in the corner there eh, that's where he sits. He's been sitting there for five hundred years, refusing to pay.

The organ pipes in the church are made of metal and reach up to the roof. My aunt said Gion Baretta plays the organ in the church and not so badly when he has a good day. I kneel in the church and look back up to the balcony when the organ plays, but can't see Gion Baretta. It's a scam, I should be able to see Gion Baretta if he's playing. Maybe he's inside the organ when he plays, but that would be strange too. After Mass I ask Nonno who says, you shouldn't be looking behind you in church, in church you look to the front with your hands joined and you don't have your fingers up your nose either. Period. I ask my aunt and she says the priest has hidden Gion Baretta—so you can't see him playing and the people at church think it's not Gion Baretta at all who's playing, but God himself at the organ.

In the church beside the priest are two altar boys. They're schoolboys with white robes on and white slippers. Round their hips they've a calving rope, the priest can use it to hold them back if one of the altar boys tries to take off. He can also tie them to the chair with the calving rope or take them for a walk after Mass, same as Fido. The altar boys have to carry the priest's things. They hold his book up when he wants to sing out of it, and they carry candles 'cause the priest's a candle person. Sometimes they even carry his smoke machine, where the priest keeps lit cigarettes. The most important thing though is that they bring the priest the cookies and the small schnapps on the golden dishware. Nonno wants us to become altar boys once we're school age. One of you will have to join a monastery anyhow and become a brother.

Fonsina has put Fridolin in the basket on the kitchen table in the Helvezia and is now drinking coffee with my aunt at the stammtisch. Fridolin's sleeping. Beside the basket with Fridolin in it is my Nonna's chicken in a metal tray. Better not leave Fridolin on the kitchen table, I say to Fonsina. Fido won't do him any harm, Fonsina says, let him sleep just. I go into the kitchen and sit on the wooden bench. I need to keep watch or Nonna will come into the kitchen and put not the chicken but Fridolin in the oven.

Gion Bi's making *poesia* for a woman no doubt, Silvana says, my mother said men make *poesia* for women to tell them they like going walkies with them and playing boccia. The women have to put the *poesia* in a wooden box and when the box is full, they're allowed to marry and make babies. I want to make *poesia* for Silvana too or I'll draw pictures for her, with bunnies in them and screw clamps. On other bits of paper, I'll draw my uncle's orange Citroën, stags' antlers and Alfons's yellow bus. I'll draw the baker with his baker's peel, Gionclau with his axe beside the Rhine, and my father and Giacasep fighting. I'll draw the whole village on lots of bits of paper and give them to Silvana, then surely I'll have enough to fill Silvana's box and she'll want to marry me. Before that though, I'll have to make a wooden box for her in Nonno's workshop so she can put the pictures in it; a beautiful wooden box with a clasp.

The band is practising marching. They're practising for Sunday and are standing in uniform on the village street. The flag bearer's at the front and right behind him is Pieder, the conductor. He has a proper conductor's baton with a cork handle. As soon as he swings the baton and says march, they all begin to move in the direction of the Helvezia and start playing. The musicians are wearing beautiful uniforms. The trousers are dark green with an orange stripe at the side, the jackets are orange with golden buttons and dark green brushes on the shoulders. The musicians don't have hats, not even Pieder, who would've had the nicest hat with huge white feathers. It's not as if we're Indians, Gion Baretta said, we're not putting the hats on. No one wanted to put the uniforms on either, no one likes them, we almost have to wear them though if the artist from the next village has already paid for them, cost a fortune after all, he says to my aunt. He'd offered to pay for the uniforms if he also got to choose them so of course everyone agreed, saying, he's a nice guy, it won't be that bad, and now we've this disgrace on our hands. He'll not be involved very much longer though, and once he's kicked the bucket we'll go back to our beautiful old uniforms, with the caps too, that is, the works; the way it should be.

Pieder marches in front of the band, swinging his baton to the beat. From time to time, he looks back and furls his eyebrows, and they all look at him wide-eyed as, red-faced, they blow into their instruments. Nonno's marching at the back, in the last row. Beside him, Anselmo is marching with the big drum. On the other side of him is Luis, with his trumpet. He has mountain boots on, like most of them, but isn't marching in step. Marches the way he wants, my aunt says, he's a talent though—that's why no one says anything. The main thing is to keep those who are still involved, there aren't that many left and won't be many more. They've even had to join up with those from the next village, or we'd no longer have a village band. Thirteen in all, so not excessively many, and Nonno can't reach the high notes any more. A few young ones would do the band good; the old ones could then finally have a rest. We clap as they march past.

Where's Fido, my brother asks my aunt. Your father's taken Fido for a walk, he's fit for nothing any more. My father has never taken Fido for a walk. He doesn't like dogs; bloody mutts, he says, good for nothing. Where'd he go, I ask my aunt. She shrugs, I don't know either. You do so, my brother says. Well, look, how can I explain it to you. Fido's old now and worn out.

Fido's tied to the fir at the edge of the forest. My father's on his stomach with his stag gun in the meadow, aiming at Fido. Fido flinches and collapses. He lies on the ground beside the tree trunk like a washrag. My father gets up. In his mouth, he has a Kiel with a yellow mouthpiece. He goes up to Fido and unties him from the tree trunk. He removes the collar, puts it in the pocket of his hunting vest, takes Fido by the neck, drags him across the meadow to the stream and throws him down the ravine. My father's gone now and Fido's lying there among the stones with his head in the water.

There's been more than a metre of snow. Caduff has come with his plough. He keeps it in the mechanic's garage and when it snows during the night he sets out. When he does, he has the orange police light on so no one's on the road when he comes. Frau Muoth should have a police light like that on the roof of her Volkswagen Beetle. As soon as it's light, all the snow has been cleared to the side so everyone can do their shopping at Marionna's and doesn't have to starve. Caduff then drives the plough back to the mechanic's garage. Holygod, watch out, the mechanic shouts when Caduff scratches the wall beside the garage door with the plough. He takes the red milling machine out of the garage. This gobbles up the snow at the edge of the road and spits it high into our garden. Now we can dig a cave, get some punch and zwieback from my mother, and move into it.

My mother isn't at home, she's gone to Glion with my brother, my father's cooking today. Fried eggs with bread are on the menu. My father stands at the cooker with the frying pan and a Kiel in his mouth. Another one, my father asks. I nod and clean my plate with the bread. My father carries the frying pan over to the table and tips the fried egg onto my plate, eat up, it'll make you big and strong. With my pocket knife, I cut away the white of the fried egg. The yoke, I eat last. Another one, my father asks when I've eaten that one up. I nod and he breaks the egg on the edge of the pan. Another one, my father asks, I nod, you've some hunger on you today, hungry as a horse you are, eat some bread too eh, the crusts as well. Right, that's enough now, my father says after the seventh fried egg, eat some bread. He puts the frying pan in the sink and sits down at the table in the corridor with his newspaper.

My aunt has a radio with a broken-off aerial. It's in the Helvezia on the buffet beside the beer glasses. In the mornings, the radio plays *ländler* music. The birthday requests come at noon. The man in the radio reads out the poems people have written for jubilarians. *Tiu natalezi sas oz festivar, da cor lein gratular*. (Your birthday today you celebrate, from our hearts we want to congratulate.) Hush, Nonna goes if someone talks during the request. It's somebody's birthday, Nonna says to my aunt, but whose just won't come to me. Even when I got up this morning I thought, it's someone's birthday today. I don't know whose it is either, my aunt says, lighting a Select. Once the requests are over, my aunt turns down the radio, which is now playing *ländler* again. Okay, I'm going up to lie down a little, Nonna says, maybe it'll come to me who. My aunt's pleased with the picture of Fido I drew for her birthday. My mother wrote happy birthday on it and me my name, bottom right, like on a Carigiet drawing.

We stand at the window, looking down onto the road, will Santa Claus be coming soon. He'll come on a sleigh pulled by his donkey with its too-big ears and bring us a big bag full of nuts, peanuts and mandarins 'cause we've not been up to any nonsense all year. He'll be here soon for sure, my mother says. From the window we can see a car that stops outside the baker's. It's Gion Baretta's red Subaru. Santa Claus gets out of the Subaru in his red costume, with his white beard in his hand, and a beautiful stick. He has a hat on his head. Santa Claus raises his hand and Gion Baretta drives off in his Subaru. My mother has put out a chair for Santa Claus. He sits down and says thank you eh. He opens his big book and says *dominus sanctus benedictus protectus* and makes the sign of the cross with his hand. We have to kneel in front of Santa Claus. Hold my stick eh, he says to my brother. Santa Claus eh, he sees everything eh, he says, and writes everything down eh, the good and the bad eh, and in the case of you two brats eh, Santa Claus had a lot of writing to do eh, or didn't he.

In Chur, they chop the peckers off uplanders with an axe, says Philip. Now now, says Frau Rorer, what kinda nonsense are ye talking, that's not nice. It's true though, says Philip, or I wouldn't be saying it. Nonsense. If he kept saying that kinda thing, there'd be no gingerbread and no cookies. When Frau Rorer goes back into the house Philip says, you wouldn't catch me setting foot in Chur if I was an uplander; much too dangerous.

In the morning, the bunnies' water has frozen over. With a screwdriver from Giacasep's, we break the ice and pour lukewarm water into the feeding trough. My mother doesn't let us go out without a cap on. In this cold, she says, the temperatures won't rise above zero till the sun returns. Herr Rorer has hung a ruler up outside his front door; he looks at it and tells us how cold it is. Minus twenty-one point two it was last night, he says, come on in, I'll make you a punch. There's fog on the lenses of his glasses. He shows us his notebook where he writes in the temperatures. What does it say here, I ask. Weather Notebook, he says and laughs, and why do you have that kind of notebook, because I'm studying how the weather is changing in the village. He's a weather student. My father isn't cold, not in the evening even; he doesn't wear a cap nor gloves either when he comes home at night with a red nose.

If you go out into the corridor at my aunt's restaurant, at the end of the corridor is a white door that is smaller than the other doors. Behind this door is a narrow room with a chair you have to stand on to reach the black phone on the wall. If someone wants to phone, my aunt has to go into the kitchen and press a red button so the phone gets some electric. *Pronto*, she calls and you can begin to dial. Even in the restaurant you can hear what people shout into the phone. When you phone you have to speak loudly and clearly so the people inside the phone can hear what you're saying.

Out on the slope in the forest clearing, we stand our skis in the snow. Tie your ski-boot laces tight, get your gaiters on, then we need to prepare the slope, my father says, placing his skis properly but not putting them on. We copy him and he helps us put our skis on, which is always a kerfuffle. Once we finally have the skis on, we climb the slope, stamping on the snow. It takes an eternity for us to get to the top, pull our caps down over our ears, put our skiing goggles with the yellow lenses on, stick our ski poles in the snow, bend our knees, and with a leap launch ourselves down the slope. Do some curves too though, my father shouts after us.

Did you not break any bones, my aunt says, laughing, when we come into the Helvezia after the downhill run in the clearing. She gives us an Ovaltine and my father a beer, a Calanda. We just have to practise braking a bit, my father says to my aunt, or they'll go into a tree on me at some point. Don't make me afraid, my aunt says. And maybe don't always go straight, but do a few curves too, or else the same thing will happen to you as happened to Pauli, my father says to us. Pauli doesn't live in our village. He just comes to the village sometimes in the yellow bus and drinks schnapps at my aunt's. He sits at the stammtisch and frowns. He only ever went straight, like a nutcase, my aunt says, and was a good skier, would've turned professional for sure like the ones on TV, and he'd no fear. And now he can't even think straight 'cause he crashed into a pylon on the ski tow.

Frau Muoth's house is snowed in. The path from the wooden fence to the front door hasn't been cleared and the shutters are closed. Frau Muoth is hibernating.

It's a bit thin, right enough, my aunt says, he could've picked a nicer fir tree, it's enough to make you feel ashamed nearly. The fir's lying behind the house. Giacasep throws it away and fetches a new one from the forest, not the finest specimen either, he says, but better at least than the cripple Nonno fetched. I wasn't able to take a proper one either, or else Nonno would notice we went back for another one. My aunt puts the new tree up in the restaurant, breaks a few branches off, and we help her decorate it. When Nonno comes, he gets himself a small beer and says, boys, come and see the Christmas tree Nonno fetched. There would've been nicer ones, eh, but Nonno fetched this one because it was trapped in the shade, growing really crooked, a poor cripple. Know what I mean. We nod. My aunt said, don't breathe a word to Nonno, *capito.*

These needles are a disgrace every year, my mother says, putting the cardboard box she fetched in Glion down on the table. In the box is a plastic Christmas tree. We're allowed to help my father assemble it. It's not so easy, he says, consulting the diagram, bloody bricolage. Bits of Christmas tree are scattered all over the living room floor. First, you have to put the trunk together, get me just the trunk parts, my father says. Once the trunk is done, the branches are next. Make sure the biggest branches are at the bottom, distributed nice and evenly, don't put all the big ones on the same side, or it'll tip over and there'll be a mess. By suppertime, the fir tree's almost ready; that's fine, my father says, almost a real Christmas tree. We gather the remaining branches up and put them in the box. A few garlands and balls now, the star at the top, and no one will notice anything. It's practical, right enough, my mother says.

Lezi has no thumb on his right hand. A black-and-white photo of him hangs above the stammtisch in the Helvezia. In the photo, he's sitting at the same table with his accordion. Before, on Friday evenings, he liked to make music with his accordion and the people all enjoyed it, Nonno says, he really did play fabulously. This very day a year ago, he went off the bridge in his van. Dead on the spot, nothing could be done. The police said he must've fallen asleep at the wheel when, early in the morning, he'd wanted to drive up after the nightshift. He was a good guy, an original, Nonno says and coughs. Went too soon. He looks at the table and says to my aunt, everyone has to go some time, and at some point there are more people in the photos round the stammtisch than sitting on the benches.

It's snowing again. The people in the village go nowhere without their shovels. Everyone has a shovel so as not to get stuck in the snow somewhere and get snowed in. Caduff does what he can with his plough, my aunt says, he's not a magician either though, so the people in the village just have to help. Giacasep is cheerful. In winter, he sells more shovels than the baker does rolls. We got a shovel too from the Night-Santa-Claus, an orange one, like my father's, with a wooden shaft and a blue plastic handle. Next year, from the Night-Santa-Claus, I want a milling machine, the kind Giacasep sells, that runs on petrol and spits the snow high in the air. A red one with a chimney and a propeller at the front like Luis's hay blower, which also tears your arm off and turns it into mince if you put your hand in.

The electric lights on the Christmas tree are on and Nonna says, but first a few songs. She strikes up and the whole family sings the Christmas song. Another one, Nonna says and my aunt says, that's probably enough for this year, it's not as if we sing so well, we need to sing another. Nonna insists though, every single verse and no leaving bits out either. When we finally reach the end of the last song we get to sit down and are given two pieces of cake and a small parcel we can only open once the prayer has been said. Inside is a gorgeous white ski helmet with red stars on it. My brother got a yellow ski helmet with black stars on it. Philip told us Santa doesn't exist, and that we only need to look in my mother's wardrobe to see if the presents are there yet, and these two helmets were there; odd right enough. Later, like every year, there's a second small parcel that Nonna brings in to us, saying Santa lost that outside on the steps. There's a bar of chocolate in it, and a five franc coin stuck on with Sellotape. It's just that this year it's a different kind of chocolate from the other years, wonder what that means, my aunt says to my mother.

Will you show us a film, Silvana asks Gion Bi. Then sit down on the sofa, he says, and already the three kings are flickering across the living room wall in their colourful clothes and with the collection in their hands. The three kings walk through the village and stop outside the Helvezia, and the black king steps forward and the others follow. Inside the Helvezia, Gion Baretta and Otto are sitting at the stammtisch, with Gionclau at the edge of the picture. My aunt's standing beside the stammtisch and takes a seat on the bench when the three kings start to sing. As they sing, you see them from up close, how their mouths open and shut and their tongues move in their mouths; you don't hear them though. The people at the stammtisch clap, and it goes black.

With our new ski helmets we're allowed up into the ski area with my mother. My mother has put on her red ski suit and queues at the ticket office. On her ears she has bushy ear warmers that look like the earmuffs we've on when we tap teeth. We wait at the valley station and have already fastened our skis. My brother waits with the skis beside the wooden bridge that goes over the small river, he slips, falls backwards and under the net and into the river. He's lost a ski and is lying on his stomach in the water, keeping his head above the water and holding onto a stone with both hands. People run over, my mother comes running up, a man's on the bridge, speaking in German as he holds his pole down, my mother screams Jeesus and drops her ear warmers, another man runs off and one climbs over the fence down into the river. In his ski boots, the water up to his knees, he walks through the river to my brother, who's still clinging to the stone. Don't let go, my mother screams, both hands up at her mouth, she still hasn't picked her ear warmers up again, don't let go, as the man finally reaches my brother and lifts him and carries him out of the river before he might've let go and disappeared with the current beneath the thick layer of snow that covers the river out as far as the lake.

Luis is sitting at the stammtisch in the Helvezia in his blue skiing jacket with the steinbock on the sleeve. Give me a quintin, he says, wiping his mouth with the back of his hand. My aunt brings him the quintin, fills his glass and puts the bottle down on the table beside the glass with the picture facing Luis. So, little chap, he says to me, alone today, where's your brother then. Fallen in the river. Had he his new helmet on at least, he asks. It fell off and is in the lake now. Aha, tell him to come to me then, I'm sure I've a spare helmet somewhere, from when I was a bobsledder. He takes a gulp of his quintin. We went down the canal in St. Moritz like savages, me at the front and Gion Baretta behind me, with his weight too, imagine, he says to my aunt, how that went. No way could you have permitted yourself any fear eh, or there'd have been no point in getting into the bobsleigh. We did it for a few years but then stopped, was hellishly expensive. Won third place in the Swiss championship in '63. Okay, give me another quintin.

Nonno's sitting in the Helvezia, at a table in the corner, doing crossword puzzles. He has his thick glasses on and round his neck he has a white towel with his initials embroidered on it. Beside him is half a litre of beer. Don't disturb him, my aunt says, drawing on her cigarette. Nonno's in training. Next week is the Swiss championship, Nonno's doing his finishing touches. If Nonno is the Swiss champion, he'll be on TV with the medal round his neck and a big trophy with champagne in it, he'll get to wear the yellow vest and our band will play the national anthem. And then, for sure, he'll be able to go to the European championship and the Olympics, and if he trains even more and only does crosswords instead of making rakes, he'll become a celebrity.

Marina's sitting in our kitchen, crying. She has her headscarf in her hand and wipes the tears from her cheeks with it. Was she out in the cold with no gloves on and now her hands are burning and making her cry, I ask my mother. She doesn't answer. Why's Marina crying, did Anselmo pull her across the kitchen floor by the hair, my brother asks. My mother has an arm round Marina and also starts crying. Marina gives my mother the headscarf. My mother sobs, you see, she says, Marina and Anselmo, she strokes Marina's back, they're returning to Italy. Are they going on holiday, *dolce far niente*. My mother stares into her coffee cup. No, they're going for good.

We look like dwarfs in our red leggings. As long as the sun's still gone, we've to put leggings on, my mother said. Okay, can we put proper trousers over them so no one sees the leggings. You got leggings on too, I ask Frau Rorer. I've tights on, Frau Rorer says, keeps ye nice and warm eh, in this cold. Would be nice if the sun returned soon, she says, a bit of sun would do people good. Minus thirteen point nine at noon, Herr Rorer says, shaking his head. When he speaks, smoke comes out of his mouth, like he was exhaling cigarette smoke. Then ciao, you lot, my brother says. Where ye going then, Herr Rorer asks with a smile. There's something we need to do still.

Behind the station, on the square beside the logs, we've cleared the snow with the shovels, ten paces on both sides. From the fountain beside Luis's house we fetch water using Luis's milking buckets, and carry it down the shortcut to behind the station. There, we pour the water onto the square. It takes a lot of buckets before the whole square's under water and we put the metal buckets back in the barn. Hold off for a day and we'll be able to play ice hockey here, with the ski helmets and with proper hockey sticks we've ordered in Giacasep's screws shop; there'll be fisticuffs with Philip too.

The apartment beneath the roof is empty now. Anselmo and Marina went yesterday, leaving the chairs and the table here. Beneath the table is one of Anselmo's socks still. On the table is an ashtray with a cigar butt. They left the key to the house in the door and the door open. Anselmo carried the cases down the stairs and put them in the trunk, *andiamo*. Giacasep stood to the side with his hands in his pockets. A lot of people from the village came to Giacasep's shop that morning, 'cause they had to buy tools, and then stood outside chatting, with clouds of smoke coming out of their mouths. *Arrivederci*, Anselmo said, lighting a Marocaine cigarette and shaking everyone's hands. Be good, Marina said, stroking our cheeks with her nice warm hand. She hadn't a headscarf on and her dark hair hung down her back like a horse's tail. Are you coming back, I asked. I'd a potato in my throat. Marina said, *sicuro*, and got in.

Make sure, my father says, you give the bunnies enough to eat. Double portions they get now. In winter they're hungrier 'cause of the cold. And they have to eat a lot now so they'll want to jump around the garden in the spring. As soon as the snow goes, we'll let them out again and they can mount each other so there'll be babies. This time, we'll watch and make sure the doe doesn't eat the babies. That's why there needs to be enough to eat, my father said, that way she'll be nice and fat and juicy.

Maybe Anselmo and Marina left, my brother says, 'cause we

poured ketchup in Anselmo's shoes. I've a bad conscience, that's why they left for sure. In Italy, no one will pour ketchup in their boots. It's your fault, my brother says, it was your idea. That night, I can't sleep. Anselmo took us by the ears 'cause we called him Gargamel, like in *The Smurfs*. When we tried to run away, I slipped on the ice outside and my brother tried to help me up but Anselmo was too swift and nearly ripped our ears off.

Nonno's standing in the workshop and leaning his hand on the planing machine. *Sacrament*, he says, wiping his brow with the tail of his beige PTT overalls. He has a lot more work now 'cause Marina's in Italy and not there to help him. Boys, he says, and we stop tapping teeth to look at him. Go over to Nonna and tell her to call your aunt. Nonno's thirsty as he's swallowed too much dust at the saw and Nonna has no more punch in the pantry. So my aunt has to bring us a bottle of punch so Nonna can make Nonno a hot punch with a dash of schnapps. It works miracles, and soon Nonno's standing up straight behind the band saw again, sawing every last thing to bits.

The Helvezia's full. The people are bunched up on the chairs. Beneath the ceiling is a sea of clouds of cigarette smoke rising from their heads. Today is the jass tournament. The winner will receive a back leg of ham and be the jass hotshot for a whole year and everyone will respect the winner and say, *salut* champ. We help my aunt to serve. We have to ask people, What would you like, then tell my aunt what they say. If someone wants crisps or cigarettes or a Kägi-Fret wafer, we can get them. It's noisy in the Helvezia. People are shouting at one another 'cause they want to win and if someone draws the wrong card, their tomato-heads curse and the spit flies across the table, their glasses fall off their noses, and my aunt has to worry that people will start breaking their half-litre beer glasses with the steinbock on them over each other's heads. Only Nonna is sitting quite calmly, moving her teeth to and fro with the regularity of a timer. She's turned her hearing aid off, my aunt says with a smirk. By the time evening falls and it's dark outside, we've heard a lot of words our mother forbids us to say. At the table in the middle sit the remaining four players; the others stand round, spurring them on like at a cow fight. In the end, Nonna draws the trump nine, wins, and Alexi curses, second yet again, bloody Nonna.

I need a break, my father says, taking his ski glasses off, and his skis as well, which he puts against the wall of the ski restaurant. Not again, we say, but my father says, come on. We pester him and finally he says, fine then, but you're only allowed to take the chair lift, I'll wait on the terrace, when you're tired, come and join me. And don't be racing like animals eh. The chair lift's old and much too slow. First, you've to queue for ages 'cause the lowlanders are on holiday and they place their poles to prevent us skipping the queue. Later, it takes a helluva long time for the chair lift finally to reach the top. We take a short cut. After the highest pylon, the smallest, we lift the bar and jump down into the deep snow. The man in the chair lift behind us goes crazy. He waves his hands, shouts and curses in German, but we don't understand that here. Here, we understand only Romansh, and not always that either.

The chair lift got stuck on our last trip up. We'd only just caught a lift when the man with the counter in his hand and the bits of spaghetti in his beard said, right that's it, and stretched the cord across. From the lift we can see my father sitting on the terrace of the mountain restaurant, drinking Calanda. We nearly reached the top, there's not far to go, such bad luck. We're two lift-lengths from the top. Here though we can't jump off 'cause it's too high and we'd break our skis. And my father would see us if he didn't happen to be chatting to the waitress at that particular moment, and then give us a torrent of abuse and lock us in the barn. It's a good thing my brother has lollipops with him, Chupa Chups, seven in all. Five Chupa Chups later, the sun has disappeared and my father's alone on the terrace. He waves to us.

We'll have to spend the night in the chair lift and will miss *Scaccia pensieri* on TV tonight, my brother says, and my mother will have to flush the rice and the beetroot down the toilet. The last of the Chupa Chups have also gone when we hear my father calling, the helicopter's on its way. My brother looks at me. Behind the blue panes in his ski glasses, his eyes look like those of a fish. I don't believe it, I say, my father's bored and joking for sure, there are no helliokopters round here. My brother says, maybe a helliokopter really is coming and it'll throw us down rucksacks with new Chupa Chups and salami and cucumber sandwiches so we don't get hungry during the night. Boys—the helicopter, my father calls. He gets up and stretches his arm out. Like that captain on his ship on TV, my father's on the terrace in his yellow Sportbeat cap, he bends over the railing and sticks his finger out. Next to him is the waitress with the green tray, holding the top of his arm tight.

It's a monster helicopter, the size of a restaurant, hovering above us in the air. It's mad, Silvana will never believe me when I tell her there are helicopters round here. Behind its glass panes are two men in grey coats. They look down, holding their levers tight. A towrope with a cage on it is hanging from the stomach of the 'copter. In it are two men with gloves and red ski suits. The 'copter lets the cage down. The man on the left in the cage shouts something in German. The cage is now so close the man with the headband can stretch and grab the bar of the chair lift and raise it. He doesn't let go of the bar and the men grab us by the arms and pull us from the chair lift up into the cage.

On the bedside table in her room Nonna has pictures of saints and crucifixes, candles and plastic bottles with blue screw-on lids. In them is her liqueur in case she gets thirsty during the night. This way, she doesn't have to get up and go into the living room, to the wall cabinet. In the evening, before she goes to bed, she fills the plastic bottles. Beside her bed, on the floor in front of the bedside table, she has a spaghetti pot without a lid that she spits into.

The Helvezia's closed for a week. My aunt has gone away on holiday. My first time away on holiday, she says, she's never yet been away on holiday. Hopefully she'll know what to do with herself, Alexi says, in the old days they'd also wanted away on holiday, would've been better staying here, that way we could've played jass, would've been just as nice as being on holiday. Let's just hope she returns. We didn't need that in the old days either, couldn't afford any further than Chur. Was in Chur a few times as a young man, and I'd have loved to have a coffee there but couldn't afford even that, or else we'd have had to walk the last bit home instead of taking the train. And nowadays everyone goes away on holiday, if possible by plane, god knows where, and you've to worry that these birds will crash out of the sky. When my aunt gets back, really brown in the face, the people in the village are glad the Helvezia's open again. Without the Helvezia I don't know what we'd do, Giachen says, but now everything's alright again. At the stammtisch the people are wide-eyed and pass round the photo of my aunt sitting on a camel.

We've put on our moon boots and wait outside Alexi's hairdressing salon till finally he comes. He's taking us to a swimming pool that's far away and where there are waves and you drink the water as you swim 'cause that's healthy. The pool's filled with water that comes straight from the mountain and is warm. In the evening, when no one's left in the pool, men come in blue overalls, caps with brims and rubber boots and fill water from the pool into green bottles with Saint Peter on them. They sell these to the restaurants and to the tourists.

After swimming, our skin looks like Nonna's. We've suddenly got old. It's 'cause of the water, Alexi said, the water stays in the mountain for a thousand years before it comes out and into the pool. We drank too much water and this is the Good Lord punishing us. Nonna will get a fright and have a heart attack when she sees us and spots we're suddenly as old as her.

I'm worn out, Alexi says after the swimming when he's finally done combing his hair, but we'll still go and have a nut croissant, you get the best in the whole canton here, you see. My brother gets a Rivella, he always drinks the red Rivella. Alexi had said as well not to play with the glass. It's too late now though, my brother's bitten into the glass and Alexi screams jesusgod and jumps up, knocking his chair over. Don't move, he says much too loudly, like when he's talking to Nonna and she hasn't switched her hearing aid on. My brother sits on the chair with the broken glass in his mouth and is wide-eyed. Alexi puts his fingers in my brother's mouth like the dentist in Disentis does. I hope my brother doesn't swallow Alexi's ring. I'm never taking you two with me again, Alexi says on every bend on the way home, furious the whole way, till we finally arrive in the village. Alexi gives us a clout round the ear, bloody rascals, and disappears into his house, banging the door.

Giacasep's outside the house, scratching the sticker with the names of Anselmo and Marina off the mailbox with a screwdriver. He takes a packet of cigarettes from his breast pocket and pops a MaryLong in his mouth. Why are you scratching the names off, I ask Giacasep. Why do you think, he says. Marina said *sicuro* when I asked her was she coming back, they still need the mailbox. No, Giacasep says, shaking his head, they're not coming back. And what if they do. They won't. But maybe they will come back again. Right, that's it.

My father has gone up to the ski slopes alone. The man from the ski lift with the counter in his hand took our season tickets and cut them in half with scissors. We're not allowed to ski any more though there's still so much snow. My father gave us pelters, serves you both right, he said, if you get caught into the bargain, *sez la cuolpa*. We skied through the forest as there are good jumps there and you can do curves round the trees. God-in-Heaven saw it though, he sees everything, Nonno said, and he phoned the man from the ski lift. When we skied through the forest the second time, the man from the ski lift with the counter in his hand skied after us. A real pursuit it was, through the whole forest, till he caught us on the slope at the edge of the forest 'cause we'd collided with tourists.

Nonno isn't in his workshop. He hasn't even cleared the new snow from the door to the workshop, and in the workshop it's as quiet as in church. He's not smoking in the boiler room either. He's overslept, my brother says. No one in the bedroom, just Nonna's spaghetti pot, full. Our punishment is to tap teeth, my father said, but if Nonno's not in the workshop, we're not tapping any. It's no fun after all, if no one's the sheriff, standing watch. Where's Nonno, we ask my aunt in the Helvezia. She closes the Romansh almanac, keeping her place with her finger. Sit down, she says, do you want an Ovaltine. One with lots of foam, my brother says. Okay, look, how can I explain it, Nonno isn't really up to it these days, Dr Tomaschett said he needs to go to hospital for a few days. Has he broken his leg. No. He has black potatoes in his chest.

My aunt bought paints in Glion so we can paint a beard on and a tash. So no one recognises us when we go through the village with cowboy hats, headscarves round our necks, vests with tassels, and revolvers. In the restaurants, we have to sing songs and throw confetti and do an act in return for cookies. Silvana's a fairy with a magic wand and a white drape. She's painted her cheeks red and her lips too with her mother's lipstick. You can have three wishes when she touches someone with her magic wand. You just mustn't tell anyone them or they won't come true. Aha, Luis says, who are these here gunmen. He's dressed up as a ski instructor. He thinks we don't recognise him in his costume.

My mother takes us to Chur where we visit Nonno in hospital. Why aren't we taking the car, I ask. The roads are icy, my mother says, and your father thinks we'll crash into a tree and smash his car. On the train, my mother reads the *NewPost* till the conductor comes and jokes with her. They talk until Chur. The conductor should actually be walking through the train, punching holes in the people's tickets, or their ears if they don't have tickets. But he sits beside my mother for the entire journey, eating zwieback.

The TV is on. Nonno's lying in his hospital bed, asleep. He has a white shirt on and looks smaller and thinner. Cables are coming from his arm. Quiet now, my mother says. She's sobbing. I've not seen Nonno sleeping before. We've to sit on the chairs beside the window. My mother fetches a vase from the cupboard, puts water in it, then the purple flowers. She puts the vase on Nonno's bedside table. Nonno moves his head to and fro. He's dreaming he's standing at his band saw and sawing through wood. Or he's dreaming he's at church and is given a whole plastic bag full of cookies by the priest 'cause occasionally he mumbles verses for the poor souls. The nurse comes into the room. We hold Nonno's hand before we go, closing the door quietly. We left the box of vitamin chocolates on top of the bed for him.

It has become warmer. We don't have to wear caps any more and the sun's almost back in the village. Alexi looks out the window of his hairdressing salon with his scissors in his hands and calls over to Otto who's behind the station, the day after tomorrow eh, at noon on the dot, the sun will shine on the station square again, just so you don't forget, we'll see then which of us was right, next year you can tell these two snots your theories. Otto stays where he is, strokes his beard, yes yes, the day after tomorrow, I wouldn't be so sure if I was you. If the sun's back again, and Alexi said it's coming back, the snow will melt, and the ice, and people won't slip and fall any more and have to go to Frau Rorer. There'll be fewer collisions in the village and the mechanic won't have any more spats about the plough with Caduff. Nonna will finally be able to sit in the garden under the apple tree again, and my father will take our bikes back out of Gaicasep's barn. The bunnies will be able to jump around the garden while we play football in shorts and Marina won't be there to grouch about us kicking the ball at her white sheets.

Quiet now, my mother says, opening the door of Nonno's hospital room. Round the bed are my aunt and Giacasep, my uncle with the bushy sideburns is there too. Nonna's sitting beside Nonno's bed on a stuffed chair, holding his hand. She has rosary beads wrapped round her wrist. Lying in the bed is Nonno. He has no hair now and looks like a washrag. His eyes are small and they shine. He only speaks quietly and slowly. The cables on his arm have gone. No one says anything. Everyone looks at Nonno, and out the window when they clean their noses. Then everything's quiet. Outside the window is a tree. The tree has no leaves. It's a big tree, like the cherry tree in our garden. From the branches of the tree hang strips of kitchen foil. They're attached to a string. There are eight strips on the tree. They move in the wind, rattling quietly. They dazzle you if you look at them and the sun shines on them. You then don't see the strip any more, you only see brightness. If you look at a strip for a long time, then look away, you see dark stains in the air. A bird flies into the windowpane. Nonno looks at Giacasep. He says, now I want a beer.

The village band has lined up behind the grave and is playing the ladybird song. There's thunder. The conductor of the village band stands in the middle. He looks down at his mountain boots. In his hand he has the baton with the cork handle. Behind him are the musicians. In front of him is the wooden cross. It is dark and on it is a white verse and numbers. Round the wooden cross lie flowers and tractor wheels. Plants are attached to the tractor wheels, and bows with golden letters. The people from the village stand round the grave. Everyone has come, only my uncle with the bushy sideburns is missing. They've joined their hands and look strict. Their clothes are black. Four men stand round the grave, two on each side, and slowly lower the coffin into the grave. The priest with the purple stole beneath the black umbrella ducks his head when Gionclau lets go of the rope too soon. Luis, on the far right with his trumpet, begins the solo.

It's raining. Silvana has put on her red cagoule and her boots. My cape is yellow. We go through the village hand-in-hand, past Giacasep's screws shop and the Usego. Past Marionna's village shop, across the small bridge and past the kiosk. Mena's sitting in her kiosk, reading the *NewPost*. She's wearing her glasses and doesn't look up. Behind her, Jesus is hanging on the cross. His right hand's broken off. We continue, past the big bridge, along the road and leave the village. When we look back a second time, the village has vanished.

ARNO CAMENISCH writes in both Rhaeto-Romanic and German. He is best known for his award-winning trilogy of novels, beginning with *The Alp* and continuing with *Behind the Station*, both published by Dalkey Archive Press.

DONAL MCLAUGHLIN was born in Northern Ireland and moved to Scotland in 1970. He is both a writer and a translator. Shortlisted for the Best Translated Book Award in 2013, he specializes in contemporary Swiss fiction. Dalkey Archive Press has also published his latest authored book, entitled *beheading the virgin mary & other stories.*

SELECTED DALKEY ARCHIVE TITLES

MICHAL AJVAZ, *The Golden Age.*
The Other City.

PIERRE ALBERT-BIROT, *Grabinoulor.*

YUZ ALESHKOVSKY, *Kangaroo.*

FELIPE ALFAU, *Chromos.*
Locos.

JOE AMATO, *Samuel Taylor's Last NIght.*

IVAN ÂNGELO, *The Celebration.*
The Tower of Glass.

ANTÓNIO LOBO ANTUNES,
Knowledge of Hell.
The Splendor of Portugal.

ALAIN ARIAS-MISSON, *Theatre of Incest.*

JOHN ASHBERY & JAMES SCHUYLER,
A Nest of Ninnies.

ROBERT ASHLEY, *Perfect Lives.*

GABRIELA AVIGUR-ROTEM,
Heatwave and Crazy Birds.

DJUNA BARNES, *Ladies Almanack.*
Ryder.

JOHN BARTH, *Letters.*
Sabbatical.

DONALD BARTHELME, *The King.*
Paradise.

SVETISLAV BASARA, *Chinese Letter.*

MIQUEL BAUÇÀ, *The Siege in the Room.*

RENÉ BELLETTO, *Dying.*

MAREK BIENCZYK, *Transparency.*

ANDREI BITOV, *Pushkin House.*

ANDREJ BLATNIK, *You Do Understand.*
Law of Desire

LOUIS PAUL BOON, *Chapel Road.*
My Little War.
Summer in Termuren.

ROGER BOYLAN, *Killoyle.*

IGNÁCIO DE LOYOLA BRANDÃO,
Anonymous Celebrity.
Zero.

BONNIE BREMSER,
Troia: Mexican Memoirs.

CHRISTINE BROOKE-ROSE,
Amalgamemnon.

BRIGID BROPHY, *In Transit.*

GERALD L. BRUNS,
Modern Poetry and the Idea of Language.

GABRIELLE BURTON, *Heartbreak Hotel.*

MICHEL BUTOR, *Degrees.*
Mobile.

G. CABRERA INFANTE, *Infante's Inferno.*
Three Trapped Tigers.

JULIETA CAMPOS,
The Fear of Losing Eurydice.

ANNE CARSON, *Eros the Bittersweet.*

ORLY CASTEL-BLOOM, *Dolly City.*

LOUIS-FERDINAND CÉLINE, *North.*
Conversations with Professor Y.
London Bridge.
Normance.

MARIE CHAIX, *T*
he Laurels of Lake Constance.

HUGO CHARTERIS, *The Tide Is Right.*

ERIC CHEVILLARD, *Demolishing Nisard.*
The Author and Me

MARC CHOLODENKO, *Mordechai Schamz.*

JOSHUA COHEN, *Witz.*

EMILY HOLMES COLEMAN,
The Shutter of Snow.

ERIC CHEVILLARD, *The Author and Me.*

ROBERT COOVER, *A Night at the Movies.*

STANLEY CRAWFORD,
Log of the S.S. The Mrs Unguentine.
Some Instructions to My Wife.

RENÉ CREVEL, *Putting My Foot in It.*

RALPH CUSACK, *Cadenza.*

NICHOLAS DELBANCO, *Sherbrookes.*
The Count of Concord.

FOR A FULL LIST OF PUBLICATIONS, VISIT: www.dalkeyarchive.com

NIGEL DENNIS, *Cards of Identity.*

PETER DIMOCK,
A Short Rhetoric for Leaving the Family.

ARIEL DORFMAN, *Konfidenz.*

COLEMAN DOWELL, *Island People.*
Too Much Flesh and Jabez.

ARKADII DRAGOMOSHCHENKO, *Dust.*

RIKKI DUCORNET,
Phosphor in Dreamland.
The Complete Butcher's Tales.
The Jade Cabinet.
The Fountains of Neptune.

WILLIAM EASTLAKE, *The Bamboo Bed.*
Castle Keep. Lyric of the Circle Heart.

JEAN ECHENOZ, *Chopin's Move.*

STANLEY ELKIN, *A Bad Man.*
Criers and Kibitzers, Kibitzers and Criers.
The Dick Gibson Show.
The Franchiser.
The Living End.
Mrs. Ted Bliss.

FRANÇOIS EMMANUEL,
Invitation to a Voyage.

PAUL EMOND, *The Dance of a Sham.*

SALVADOR ESPRIU,
Ariadne in the Grotesque Labyrinth.

LESLIE A. FIEDLER,
Love and Death in the American Novel.

JUAN FILLOY, *Op Oloop.*

ANDY FITCH, *Pop Poetics.*

GUSTAVE FLAUBERT,
Bouvard and Pécuchet.

KASS FLEISHER, *Talking out of School.*

JON FOSSE, *Aliss at the Fire.*
Melancholy.

FORD MADOX FORD,
The March of Literature.

MAX FRISCH, *I'm Not Stiller.*
Man in the Holocene.

CARLOS FUENTES, *Christopher Unborn.*
Distant Relations.
Terra Nostra.
Where the Air Is Clear.

TAKEHIKO FUKUNAGA, *Flowers of Grass.*

WILLIAM GADDIS, JR., *The Recognitions.*

JANICE GALLOWAY, *Foreign Parts.*
The Trick Is to Keep Breathing.

WILLIAM H. GASS,
Cartesian Sonata and Other Novellas.
Life Sentences
The Tunnel.
The World Within the Word
Willie Masters' Lonesome Wife.

GÉRARD GAVARRY, *Hoppla! 1 2 3.*

ETIENNE GILSON,
The Arts of the Beautiful.
Forms and Substances in the Arts.

C. S. GISCOMBE, *Giscome Road.*
Here.

DOUGLAS GLOVER,
Bad News of the Heart.

WITOLD GOMBROWICZ,
A Kind of Testament.

PAULO EMÍLIO SALES GOMES,
P's Three Women.

GEORGI GOSPODINOV, *Natural Novel.*

JUAN GOYTISOLO, *Count Julian.*
Juan the Landless.
Makbara.
Marks of Identity.

HENRY GREEN, *Blindness.*
Concluding.
Doting.
Nothing.

JACK GREEN, *Fire the Bastards!*

JIŘÍ GRUŠA, *The Questionnaire.*

MELA HARTWIG,
Am I a Redundant Human Being?

JOHN HAWKES, *The Passion Artist.*
Whistlejacket.

ELIZABETH HEIGHWAY, ED., *Contemporary Georgian Fiction.*

ALEKSANDAR HEMON, ED., *Best European Fiction.*

AIDAN HIGGINS, *Balcony of Europe.*
Blind Man's Bluff.
Bornholm Night-Ferry.
Flotsam and Jetsam.
Langrishe, Go Down.
Scenes from a Receding Past.

KEIZO HINO, *Isle of Dreams.*

KAZUSHI HOSAKA, *Plainsong.*

ALDOUS HUXLEY, *Antic Hay.*
Crome Yellow.
Point Counter Point.
Those Barren Leaves.
Time Must Have a Stop.

NAOYUKI II, *The Shadow of a Blue Cat.*

DRAGO JANČAR, *The Tree with No Name.*

MIKHEIL JAVAKHISHVILI, *Kvachi.*

GERT JONKE, *The Distant Sound.*
Homage to Czerny.
The System of Vienna.

JACQUES JOUET, *Mountain R. Savage.*
Upstaged.

MIEKO KANAI, *The Word Book.*

YORAM KANIUK, *Life on Sandpaper.*

ZURAB KARUMIDZE, *Dagny.*

JOHN KELLY, *From Out of the City.*

HUGH KENNER, *Flaubert.*
Joyce and Beckett: The Stoic Comedians.
Joyce's Voices.

DANILO KIŠ, *The Attic.*
The Lute and the Scars.
Psalm 44.
A Tomb for Boris Davidovich.

ANITA KONKKA, *A Fool's Paradise.*

GEORGE KONRÁD, *The City Builder.*

TADEUSZ KONWICKI, *A Minor Apocalypse.*
The Polish Complex.

ANNA KORDZAIA-SAMADASHVILI,
Me, Margarita.

MENIS KOUMANDAREAS, *Koula.*

ELAINE KRAF, *The Princess of 72nd Street.*

JIM KRUSOE, *Iceland.*

AYSE KULIN,
Farewell: A Mansion in Occupied Istanbul.

EMILIO LASCANO TEGUI,
On Elegance While Sleeping.

ERIC LAURRENT, *Do Not Touch.*

VIOLETTE LEDUC, *La Bâtarde.*

EDOUARD LEVÉ, *Autoportrait.*
Suicide. Works.

MARIO LEVI, *Istanbul Was a Fairy Tale.*

DEBORAH LEVY, *Billy and Girl.*

JOSÉ LEZAMA LIMA, *Paradiso.*

ROSA LIKSOM, *Dark Paradise.*

OSMAN LINS, *Avalovara.*
The Queen of the Prisons of Greece.

FLORIAN LIPUŠ, *The Errors of Young Tjaž.*

GORDON LISH, *Peru.*

ALF MACLOCHLAINN, *Out of Focus.*
Past Habitual
The Corpus in the Library.

RON LOEWINSOHN, *Magnetic Field(s).*

YURI LOTMAN, *Non-Memoirs.*

D. KEITH MANO, *Take Five.*

MINA LOY, *Stories and Essays of Mina Loy.*

MICHELINE AHARONIAN MARCOM,
A Brief History of Yes.
The Mirror in the Well.

BEN MARCUS, *The Age of Wire and String.*

WALLACE MARKFIELD,
Teitlebaum's Window.

DAVID MARKSON, *Reader's Block.*
Wittgenstein's Mistress.

CAROLE MASO, *AVA.*

LADISLAV MATEJKA & KRYSTYNA POMORSKA, EDS., *Readings in Russian Poetics: Formalist & Structuralist Views.*

HARRY MATHEWS, *Cigarettes.*
The Conversions.
The Human Country.
The Journalist.
My Life in CIA.
Singular Pleasures.
The Sinking of the Odradek.
Stadium.
Tlooth.

HISAKI MATSUURA, *Triangle.*

DONAL MCLAUGHLIN, *beheading the virgin mary, and other stories.*

JOSEPH MCELROY, *Night Soul and Other Stories.*

ABDELWAHAB MEDDEB, *Talismano.*

GERHARD MEIER, *Isle of the Dead.*

HERMAN MELVILLE, *The Confidence-Man.*

AMANDA MICHALOPOULOU, *I'd Like.*

STEVEN MILLHAUSER, *The Barnum Museum.*
In the Penny Arcade.

RALPH J. MILLS, JR., *Essays on Poetry.*

MOMUS, *The Book of Jokes.*

CHRISTINE MONTALBETTI, *The Origin of Man.*
Western.

OLIVE MOORE, *Spleen.*

NICHOLAS MOSLEY, *Accident.*
Assassins.
Catastrophe Practice.
A Garden of Trees.
Hopeful Monsters.
Imago Bird.
Inventing God.
Look at the Dark.
Metamorphosis.
Natalie Natalia.
Serpent.
Time at War.

WARREN MOTTE, *Fables of the Novel: French Fiction since 1990.*
Fiction Now: The French Novel in the 21st Century.
Mirror Gazing.
Oulipo: A Primer of Potential Literature.

GERALD MURNANE, *Barley Patch.*
Inland.

YVES NAVARRE, *Our Share of Time.*
Sweet Tooth.

DOROTHY NELSON, *In Night's City.*
Tar and Feathers.

ESHKOL NEVO, *Homesick.*

WILFRIDO D. NOLLEDO, *But for the Lovers.*

BORIS A. NOVAK, *The Master of Insomnia.*

FLANN O'BRIEN, *At Swim-Two-Birds.*
The Best of Myles.
The Dalkey Archive.
The Hard Life.
The Poor Mouth.
The Third Policeman.

CLAUDE OLLIER, *The Mise-en-Scène.*
Wert and the Life Without End.

PATRIK OUŘEDNÍK, *Europeana.*
The Opportune Moment, 1855.

BORIS PAHOR, *Necropolis.*

FERNANDO DEL PASO, *News from the Empire.*
Palinuro of Mexico.

ROBERT PINGET, *The Inquisitory.*
Mahu or The Material.
Trio.

MANUEL PUIG, *Betrayed by Rita Hayworth.*
The Buenos Aires Affair.
Heartbreak Tango.

RAYMOND QUENEAU, *The Last Days.*
Odile.
Pierrot Mon Ami.
Saint Glinglin.

ANN QUIN, *Berg.*
Passages.
Three.
Tripticks.

ISHMAEL REED, *The Free-Lance Pallbearers.*
The Last Days of Louisiana Red.
Ishmael Reed: The Plays.
Juice!
The Terrible Threes.
The Terrible Twos.
Yellow Back Radio Broke-Down.

JASIA REICHARDT,
15 Journeys Warsaw to London.

JOÃO UBALDO RIBEIRO,
House of the Fortunate Buddhas.

JEAN RICARDOU, *Place Names.*

RAINER MARIA RILKE,
The Notebooks of Malte Laurids Brigge.

JULIÁN RÍOS, The House of Ulysses.
Larva. A Midsummer Night's Babel.
Poundemonium.

ALAIN ROBBE-GRILLET,
A Sentimental Novel.

AUGUSTO ROA BASTOS, *I the Supreme.*

DANIËL ROBBERECHTS,
Arriving in Avignon.

JEAN ROLIN,
The Explosion of the Radiator Hose.

OLIVIER ROLIN, *Hotel Crystal.*

ALIX CLEO ROUBAUD, *Alix's Journal.*

JACQUES ROUBAUD,
The Form of a City Changes Faster, Alas, Than the Human Heart.
The Great Fire of London.
Hortense in Exile.
Hortense Is Abducted.
Mathematics: The Plurality of Worlds of Lewis.
Some Thing Black.

RAYMOND ROUSSEL, *Impressions of Africa.*

VEDRANA RUDAN, *Night.*

TOMAŽ ŠALAMUN, *Soy Realidad.*

LYDIE SALVAYRE, *The Company of Ghosts.*
The Lecture.
The Power of Flies.

LUIS RAFAEL SÁNCHEZ,
Macho Camacho's Beat.

SEVERO SARDUY, *Cobra & Maitreya.*

NATHALIE SARRAUTE,
Do You Hear Them?
Martereau.
The Planetarium.

STIG SÆTERBAKKEN, *Siamese.*
Self-Control.
Through the Night

ARNO SCHMIDT, *Collected Novellas.*
Collected Stories.
Nobodaddy's Children.
Two Novels.

ASAF SCHURR, *Motti.*

GAIL SCOTT, *My Paris.*

DAMION SEARLS,
What We Were Doing and Where We Were Going.

JUNE AKERS SEESE,
Is This What Other Women Feel Too?

BERNARD SHARE, *Inish.*
Transit.

VIKTOR SHKLOVSKY, *Bowstring.*
Literature and Cinematography.
Theory of Prose.
Third Factory.
Zoo, or Letters Not about Love.

PIERRE SINIAC, *The Collaborators.*

KJERSTI A. SKOMSVOLD, *The Faster I Walk, the Smaller I Am.*

JOSEF ŠKVORECKÝ, *The Engineer ofHuman Souls.*

GILBERT SORRENTINO, *Aberration of Starlight.*
Blue Pastoral.
Crystal Vision.
Imaginative Qualities of Actual Things.
Mulligan Stew.
Red the Fiend.
Splendide-Hôtel.
Under the Shadow.

W. M. SPACKMAN, *The Complete Fiction.*

ANDRZEJ STASIUK, *Dukla.*
Fado.

GERTRUDE STEIN, *The Making of Americans.*
A Novel of Thank You.

LARS SVENDSEN, *A Philosophy of Evil.*

PIOTR SZEWC, *Annihilation.*

GONÇALO M. TAVARES, *Jerusalem.*
Joseph Walser's Machine.
Learning to Pray in the Age of Technique.

LUCIAN DAN TEODOROVICI, *Our Circus Presents . . .*

NIKANOR TERATOLOGEN, *Assisted Living.*

STEFAN THEMERSON, *Hobson's Island.*
The Mystery of the Sardine.
Tom Harris.

TAEKO TOMIOKA, *Building Waves.*

JOHN TOOMEY, *Sleepwalker.*

JEAN-PHILIPPE TOUSSAINT, *The Bathroom.*
Monsieur.
Reticence.
Running Away.
Self-Portrait Abroad.
The Truth about Marie.

DUMITRU TSEPENEAG, *Hotel Europa.*
The Necessary Marriage.
Pigeon Post.
Vain Art of the Fugue.

ESTHER TUSQUETS, *Stranded.*

DUBRAVKA UGRESIC, *Lend Me Your Character.*
Thank You for Not Reading.

TOR ULVEN, *Replacement.*

MATI UNT, *Brecht at Night.*
Diary of a Blood Donor.
Things in the Night.

ÁLVARO URIBE & OLIVIA SEARS, EDS., *Best of Contemporary Mexican Fiction.*

ELOY URROZ, *Friction.*
The Obstacles.

LUISA VALENZUELA, *Dark Desires and the Others.*
He Who Searches.

PAUL VERHAEGHEN, *Omega Minor.*

BORIS VIAN, *Heartsnatcher.*

LLORENÇ VILLALONGA, *The Dolls' Room.*

TOOMAS VINT, *An Unending Landscape.*

ORNELA VORPSI, *The Country Where No One Ever Dies.*

AUSTRYN WAINHOUSE, *Hedyphagetica.*

CURTIS WHITE, *America's Magic Mountain.*
The Idea of Home.
Memories of My Father Watching TV.
Requiem.

DIANE WILLIAMS, *Excitability: Selected Stories.*
Romancer Erector.

DOUGLAS WOOLF, *Wall to Wall.*
Ya! & John-Juan.

JAY WRIGHT, *Polynomials and Pollen.*
The Presentable Art of Reading Absence.

FOR A FULL LIST OF PUBLICATIONS, VISIT: www.dalkeyarchive.com

PHILIP WYLIE, *Generation of Vipers.*

MARGUERITE YOUNG,
Angel in the Forest.
Miss MacIntosh, My Darling.

REYOUNG, *Unbabbling.*

VLADO ŽABOT, *The Succubus.*

ZORAN ŽIVKOVIĆ , *Hidden Camera.*

LOUIS ZUKOFSKY, *Collected Fiction.*

VITOMIL ZUPAN, *Minuet for Guitar.*

SCOTT ZWIREN, *God Head.*